TIME Basic Words 888

美國《時代雜誌》全球獨家授權

大師推薦

托福滿分 旋元佑
英文榜首 張嘉倩
字彙專家 梁民康

單字記憶法大公開

姜敬寬 博士
▼台大新聞研究所客座教授
▼任職美國《時代雜誌》編輯三十餘年

成露茜 博士
▼台大城鄉研究所客座教授
▼美國加州大學洛杉磯分校 (UCLA) 永久正教授

單

中級字彙

挑

熟讀888個單字

輕鬆挑戰全民英檢

經典傳訊
Classic Communications Co.

NOTICE

Preface

For nearly 75 years, TIME has reported on the latest trends in world politics, science and culture for an informed audience around the world. It sets the agenda for discussion of important issues for influential citizens in every nation.

Similarly, its editors and writers have long set the standard for elegance and clarity of expression in English. Their way with words has been widely imitated but perhaps never improved upon. Much of the pleasure for TIME's most faithful readers comes from the magazine's unique way of telling a story in fresh, lively terms.

So to learn how to communicate not just clearly but elegantly, the vocabulary and expressions employed in TIME make a great place to start. We are delighted to make available to native Chinese-language readers these unique guides to the language of TIME. We are confident these will be a valuable aide to the user's understanding, not just of what is reported in TIME each week, but of all the rapid changes in the world around us.

John Marcom

Publisher - Asia, TIME

《時代雜誌》亞洲區發行人

發行人序

美國《時代雜誌》(TIME Magazine) 每週發行全世界一百八十餘個國家、六百萬冊，傳閱率達三千萬人次，是全球最權威、發行量最大的新聞雜誌。TIME 以其客觀的立論、精闢的分析，深獲全世界各國政經領袖、學者專家、知識份子、企業主管的一致推崇。

創刊於一九二三年的 TIME，七十八年來始終是全球知識份子的 leading magazine。對中國的知識份子，甚而對中國近代的命運，TIME 亦發揮了深遠閎大的影響。但由於語言難度及文化差異的隔閡，使得古往今來多少想閱讀 TIME 的華人，往往心有餘而力未逮。

現在，全球第一套由時代集團 (TIME Inc.) 獨家授權經典傳訊 (Classic Communications Co.)，並共同規畫的「時代經典系列」(TIME Classic Series) 將在全球華語國家陸續出版。

本系列第一套書為《時代經典用字》(TIME Classic Words)，本套書共四本，分別為政治篇、科技篇、商業篇及人文篇。《時代經典用字》是所有想培養國際視野的讀者之必備寶典。四本書中的每一個字皆代表一個重要國際事件、一個重要科技演進、一個重要財經觀點、一個重要文化思潮。經由經典傳訊資深主筆群將事件發生背景做充分注解，並賦予「時代意義」——不但來自《時代雜誌》，更來自我們身處的大時代。

　　本系列第二套書爲「單挑系列」(TIME Key Words)，以TIME 常用各類型單字及精彩例句、文章爲題材，循序推出相關單字書。

　　本系列第三套書爲「片挑系列」(TIME Key Phrases)，以TIME 常用各類型片語及精彩例句、文章爲題材，循序推出相關的片語書。

　　本系列第四套書爲「閱讀系列」(TIME Key Reports)，以TIME 歷年來精彩的文章、重要的文獻爲閱讀文本，因爲閱讀好文章及名家作品是增進英文實力的不二法門。

　　「時代經典系列」不但是閱讀 TIME 的最佳輔助學習工具，同時見證了二十世紀近百年來美式英語的變遷，以及美國經濟、社會的發展，是身處二十一世紀「無國界社會」的現代華人提升競爭力的知識寶典。

經典傳訊發行人

How I Built Up an English Vocabulary

I began learning English during my sixth-grade summer, before starting junior high school. The missionaries at the church next to my house started a free English class for kids on the block, teaching the letters, with a demonstrative word attached to each letter. Therefore, like many other people, I started building an English vocabulary as soon as I started learning English.

Throughout junior and senior high school, I relied primarily on English textbooks for new words. At that age I had an excellent memory. Whenever the teacher started a new lesson, I would have memorized all the new words in it before class was dismissed. I had to, for the exams. But then again, that kind of memorization was vital, for it laid a solid foundation for future work. Later, when I became an English major at National Taiwan Normal University, I had to do a lot of reading, and there was no time to look up every unfamiliar word, much less memorize it. I found it easy to handle the coursework, primarily because the foundation was good.

Currently, as Chief Editorial Writer for *TIME for Students*, I am responsible for keeping the English in the magazine correct and also appropriate in terms of difficulty. All the vocabulary words in every issue are carefully screened. Now Classic Communications has screened again all the contents of *TIME for Students* from the very first issue to the present, and has selected 888 vocabulary words for this *TIME Basic Words 888*. These are the most important core vocabulary words. If you like to lay down a sound foundation for your English abilities, or need to prepare for exams, school admission, or employment, *TIME Basic Words 888* is your best choice.

Hsuan Yuanyu
Chief Editorial Writer
Classic Communications Co.

我學單字的經驗

最早接觸英文，是在小學升初中那個暑假。我家隔壁教會的傳教士為社區兒童開了個免費的英文班，教的是二十六個英文字母，各配上一個單字。所以，我學單字的經驗和許多人一樣，是打從一開始接觸英文就開始了。

在初中、高中階段，我學的單字主要來自英文課本。年紀輕、記憶力強，每上一課新的英文，我大概在下課前就先把這一課的單字背起來了。那是為了應付考試不得不背，但也是最重要的打基礎的工作。進了師大英語系之後，要做大量的閱讀，不再有時間慢慢查單字、背單字。能夠讀得輕鬆愉快，主要是因為從前基礎打得好。

我現在擔任 TIME for Students 雜誌的總主筆，要負責審核雜誌中的英文，確保它正確無誤以及難度適中。每一期的單字都經過仔細的篩選。如今經典傳訊把 TIME for Students 創刊以來的內容重新篩選，挑出 888 個單字編成這本《TIME 單挑中級字彙 888》。這裏面的單字可以說是最重要的核心單字。如果你想為英文打下良好的基礎，或者要準備考試、升學、就業，《TIME 單挑中級字彙 888》會是你明智的選擇。

經典傳訊總主筆

旋元佑

背英文單字的基本觀念

台灣人的英文單字程度低落原因為何？第一，懶惰不背單字。第二，背單字方法錯誤。以下分述之。

懶惰的人分兩種，一種是根本不在乎，認為自己用不到英文，自然不背單字。在世界四分之三以上的資訊以英文形式流通的現在，我們只能給這種人深深的祝福。另一種人有心學英文，卻被無數不實廣告欺騙，以為「一個禮拜」，「一個月」就能精通會話、閱讀，聽懂國家地理頻道、CNN，變成英文全才。他們根本來不及背單字嘛！

台灣的莘莘學子，應該多數屬於後者「背單字方法錯誤」。首先，台灣的中學英語教科書課文與考試題目，泰半由本地教師自行撰寫或從名著改寫，許多字的用法根本就是錯的，卻成為「標準英文」，學生成為以訛傳訛的受害者。另外，一般單字書都錯誤地緊守「一字一義」原則，造成學生在看到不同用法時無法理解。再者，許多學過、背過的單字從來派不上用場，等於「廢字」。看了本文的讀者，腦子裡一定有上千個「廢字」。

歸納以上所述，「用原味例句學單字用法」、「一字多義」、「出現率高的字先背」才是背單字的正確觀念。

經典傳訊資深主筆

英文榜首背單字的方法

單字是英文聽說讀寫的基礎，不過如果背單字只是「單單背一個字」就太可惜了。

其實背單字也可以聽說讀寫一起來的。

1. 聽，聽單字書附的 CD，熟悉正確的發音。

2. 說，跟著念，並多說幾次。

3. 讀，用眼睛看，並熟記例句，確實了解單字的用法。

4. 寫，自己用單字造一個句子，並盡量在寫文章時，將新學的單字用出來。

而如果不想背了又忘，除了背單字書外，一定還要加上大量閱讀。如果你的英文閱讀量夠大，開始背單字後，就會發現一件很奇妙的事，那就是這星期背的字，下星期就會在所讀的文章中出現，這是因為剛開始背單字是從最常用的單字開始，這些字原本就常出現在許多文章中，而在文章中看到新認識的朋友，驚喜之餘，也會對這個字留下更深的印象。

有了穩固的基本字彙基礎，如果想更上一層樓，背難度更高的字，就要借助字根字首的方法了，不過，先背完《TIME 單挑中級字彙 888》這本單字書再說吧！

英文榜首

張嘉倩

編輯緣起

　　TIME 是全球最權威、發行量最大的新聞雜誌，用字遣詞一直是嚴謹而富創意的。時代集團獨家授權的 TIME for Students《時代新鮮人》則承續著《時代雜誌》一貫的品質，同樣屬於新聞性、知識性的雜誌，字彙難度雖不若 TIME，屬於中級單字，然而行筆活潑，在吸收新知的同時掌握關鍵字的用法，是最適合高中、高職學生閱讀的英語學習雜誌。

　　由於 TIME for Students《時代新鮮人》用字趨於生活化、文筆生動而直接，文章取材新奇生動、引人入勝，與全民英檢中級測驗、大學入學考試的出題方向不謀而合，更加強了讀者對它的信心與期待。

■ 系出名門・信心滿分

　　《TIME 單挑 1000》自一九九七年出版以來，已嘉惠無數的英語學習者，有鑑於此，我們相信一本定位明確、挑字精準的單字書絕對是備受讀者期待的。我們從 TIME for Students《時代新鮮人》自創刊以來的雜誌裡挑出了 888 個解讀一般文章必備的關鍵字，編輯成《TIME 單挑中級字彙 888》，這些單字也是高中、高職學生必須具備的字彙，絕對是左右考場、職場的獨門武器。

■ 單字解釋・無「獨」有「偶」

　　《TIME 單挑中級字彙 888》與《TIME 單挑 1000》一脈相

著分類清晰、容易閱讀的優點。888 個單字依詞性分為形容詞／副詞、動詞、名詞三大類；各類單字依字母順序編排。每個單字除了常用字義與音標之外，還有最能代表該單字用法的例句。此外，《TIME 單挑中級字彙 888》裡的單字字義是以使用率作為註釋原則的：

- 單字最常用的字義只有一個時
  例如： effective [ə`fɛktɪv] (a.) 有效的
- 單字有兩個最常用的相近字義時，用「逗號」區隔
  例如： elegant [`ɛləgənt] (a.) 精緻的，優雅的
- 單字有兩個最常用的不同字義時，用「分號」區隔
  例如： profile [`profaɪl] (n.) 人物簡介；側面

這樣的單字註解方式是希望讀者能夠學習到單字的正確用法，靈活運用不犯錯。

■ 單字分兩級‧效率擺中間

《TIME 單挑中級字彙 888》裡的單字難度相當於全民英檢測驗 (GEPT) 的中級到中高級。為方便不同學習目標的讀者，提高學習效率，特地由經典傳訊考題研究小組為本書所有單字分級。在單字前標示「◆」的單字為中高級單字，沒有標示「◆」者為中級單字。希望藉此能讓讀者掌握最關鍵、最重要的單字，節省準備時間，提高學習效率。

■ 升學就業 · 無往不利

　　英文的強勢不僅在媒體上展現，也是升學考試的共同科目，近來更是職場徵才的重要參考指標。本書的單字難度相當於高中、高職畢業生應該具備的字彙能力，參考下列表格，你可以清楚知道讀完本書後的字彙能力相當於其他考試的哪個級數。在面對嚴峻的考場試煉前，本書中由英語教學專家 Andrew E. Bennett 設計的字彙測驗可以讓你熟悉考試題型，不論是大學入學考試、全民英檢測驗或是多益測驗，走出考場後，想升學的可以準備去註冊，要就業的就準備報到吧！

TIME 單挑 中級字彙 888	程度相當於		
	全民英檢 GEPT	多益 TOEIC	托福 TOEFL
	中級測驗（高中程度） 中高級測驗（大學程度）	420 ～ 650 分	電腦考試 140 ～ 190 分 傳統考試 480 ～ 550 分

使用說明

標示「♦」為中高級
單字,未標示「♦」
者則為中級單字

中文字義,為此單字
最常用的字義解釋

所介紹單字　　音標　詞性

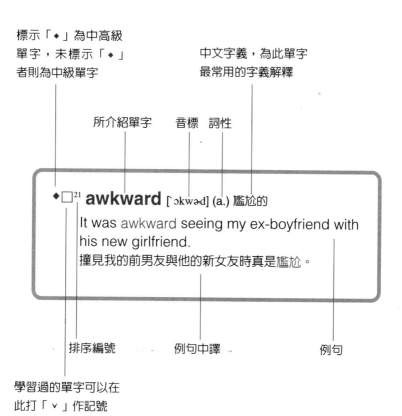

♦□²¹ **awkward** [ˋɔkwəd] (a.) 尷尬的

It was awkward seeing my ex-boyfriend with his new girlfriend.
撞見我的前男友與他的新女友時真是尷尬。

排序編號　　　　例句中譯　　　　　例句

學習過的單字可以在
此打「ˇ」作記號

「字」我挑戰

在熟讀每個單元的單字後，相信你已經掌握了每個單字的意義與用法，單元最後的「字」我挑戰部分，就是你單挑自己的地方。希望你在十分鐘內做完一回試題，並對照本書第 290 頁的答案。

建議你將答錯的題目，在下面表格中的圓圈上作記號，這樣一來，你的單字實力累積成果就一目了然了，更可以清楚知道自己哪種詞性的單字實力比較弱，日後複習的時候，可以直接翻到你較弱的部分特別加強。

挑戰「字」我　戰績表

詞性	回數	第1題	第2題	第3題	第4題	第5題	第6題	第7題	第8題	第9題	第10題	第11題	第12題
形容詞／副詞	「字」我挑戰 1	○	○	○	○	○	○	○	○	○	○	○	○
	「字」我挑戰 2	○	○	○	○	○	○	○	○	○	○	○	○
	「字」我挑戰 3	○	○	○	○	○	○	○	○	○	○	○	○
動詞	「字」我挑戰 4	○	○	○	○	○	○	○	○	○	○	○	○
	「字」我挑戰 5	○	○	○	○	○	○	○	○	○	○	○	○
	「字」我挑戰 6	○	○	○	○	○	○	○	○	○	○	○	○
	「字」我挑戰 7	○	○	○	○	○	○	○	○	○	○	○	○
名詞	「字」我挑戰 8	○	○	○	○	○	○	○	○	○	○	○	○
	「字」我挑戰 9	○	○	○	○	○	○	○	○	○	○	○	○
	「字」我挑戰 10	○	○	○	○	○	○	○	○	○	○	○	○
	「字」我挑戰 11	○	○	○	○	○	○	○	○	○	○	○	○

CONTENTS

完整版 CD I~III 以每兩頁（八個單字）為一個音軌，不足八個字則自成一個音軌。
單字精簡複習 CD IV 則以每個 Chapter 為一個音軌。

TIME

Basic Words 888

形容詞／副詞

Chapter 1

1~80

共 240 字

- abandoned 被拋棄的
- addicted 上癮的
- adorable 可愛的
- advanced 先進的
- adventurous 愛冒險的
- affordable 買得起的，負擔得起的
- aggressive 積極的
- agricultural 農業的
- alarming 驚人的
- alien 外星的
- alternative 另類的；代替的
- ancient 古代的，古老的
- anonymous 匿名的
- anxious 渴望的；焦慮的
- apparently 顯然地；似乎
- appropriate 適當的
- artificial 人造的
- astounding 令人震驚的
- automatically 自動地
- available 可取得的
- awkward 尷尬的
- beloved 受人喜愛的
- bewildering 令人困惑的
- bizarre 怪異的
- bold 大膽的
- brilliant 聰穎的；燦爛的
- carefree 無憂無慮的

- caring 關心別人的
- cautious 謹慎的，小心的
- chain 連鎖的
- challenging 有挑戰性的
- chilling 可怕的
- compelling 令人無法抵抗的
- concerned 憂慮的，擔心的
- concise 簡潔的
- confidential 機密的
- consecutive 連續的
- controversial 引起爭議的
- corrupt 腐敗的，貪污的
- countless 數不清的，無數的
- crude 粗魯的，無禮的
- cultural 文化的
- curious 好奇的
- curly 捲髮的；捲曲的
- current 目前的
- currently 目前
- deceitful 好欺詐的
- definitely 絕對地
- demanding 要求嚴格的
- densely 稠密地
- desperate 迫切的
- devoted 熱愛的；忠實的
- disgusting 令人厭惡的
- distinct 清楚的
- distinctive 獨特的

- dramatically 大幅地
- dual 雙重的
- dull 枯燥的，呆板的
- **eager 熱切的**
- easygoing 隨和的
- effective 有效的
- efficient 有效率的
- electronic 電子的
- elegant 優雅的，精緻的
- enormous 龐大的
- enterprising 有進取心的
- enthusiastic 熱中的
- essential 必要的；基本的
- evasive 躲避的，逃避的
- eventually 最後，終於
- exactly 完全地
- exclusive 獨家的
- exhausting 使人筋疲力盡的
- exhilarated 興奮的
- explosive 爆炸性的
- expressive 富於表情的
- extraordinary 非凡的
- **faint 微弱的**
- fairly 相當地
- fashionable 流行的

□¹ **abandoned** [əˋbændənd] (a.) 被拋棄的

I like walking around abandoned old houses.
我喜歡在廢棄的老房子附近走走。

□² **addicted** [əˋdɪktɪd] (a.) 上癮的

Don't you ever smoke, or you may get addicted.
千萬不要吸菸，不然你可能會上癮。

□³ **adorable** [əˋdorəbl] (a.) 可愛的

Everybody finds John's kid sister simply adorable.
大家都覺得約翰的小妹妹可愛極了。

□⁴ **advanced** [ədˋvænst] (a.) 先進的

Our company is equipped with the most advanced computers.
我們公司有最先進的電腦。

abandoned　　addicted　　adorable　　advanced

□⁵ **adventurous** [əd`vɛntʃərəs] (a.) 愛冒險的

Tom's adventurous nature has taken him to every country in the world.
湯姆愛冒險的天性已經讓他走遍世界各國。

□⁶ **affordable** [ə`fɔrdəbl] (a.) 買得起的，負擔得起的

I found an affordable way to travel: by bicycle!
我找到一個負擔得起的旅行方法：騎腳踏車！

□⁷ **aggressive** [ə`grɛsɪv] (a.) 積極的

The company has launched an aggressive campaign for its new product.
這家公司為新產品展開了積極的宣傳活動。

□⁸ **agricultural** [ˌægrɪ`kʌltʃərəl] (a.) 農業的

America exports millions of tons of agricultural produce every year.
美國每年對外輸出數百萬噸的農產品。

N
O
P
Q
R
S
T
U
V
W
X
Y
Z

adventurous | affordable | aggressive | agricultural

□⁹ **alarming** [əˋlɑrmɪŋ] (a.) 驚人的

The number of people with the AIDS virus is increasing at an alarming rate.
感染愛滋病毒的人數以驚人的比例成長。

□¹⁰ **alien** [ˋeljən] (a.) 外星的

Do you believe in alien beings from outer space?
你相信有外太空來的外星生物嗎？

□¹¹ **alternative** [ɔlˋtɝnətɪv] (a.) 另類的；代替的

Alternative medicine cures diseases just like traditional medicine.
另類醫療就和傳統醫療一樣也能治病。

□¹² **ancient** [ˋenʃənt] (a.) 古代的，古老的

Gunpowder was invented in ancient China.
火藥是在古代中國發明的。

| alarming | alien | alternative | ancient |

□¹³ **anonymous** [əˋnɑnəməs] (a.) 匿名的

The protestors mailed anonymous letters to the government.
抗議者寄匿名信給政府。

□¹⁴ **anxious** [ˋæŋkʃəs] (a.) 渴望的；焦慮的

I enjoyed my vacation, but I'm anxious to get back to work.
我的假期很愉快，但現在我渴望回去工作。

□¹⁵ **apparently** [əˋpærəntlɪ] (adv.) 顯然地；似乎

He apparently doesn't want to work here anymore.
他顯然不想在這裡工作下去。

□¹⁶ **appropriate** [əˋproprɪɪt] (a.) 適當的

The young man is waiting for the appropriate moment to propose to the lady.
這名年輕人在等待適當的時機向這個小姐求婚。

anonymous　anxious　apparently　appropriate

□¹⁷ **artificial** [ˌɑrtəˋfɪʃəl] (a.) 人造的

These artificial flowers look like real ones.
這些人造花看起來像真的一樣。

◆□¹⁸ **astounding** [əˋstaʊndɪŋ] (a.) 令人震驚的

There were several reasons for the
astounding defeat of the ruling party.
執政黨令人震驚的失敗有好幾個原因。

□¹⁹ **automatically** [ˌɔtəˋmætɪklɪ] (adv.) 自動地

Streetlights automatically turn on when it
gets dark.
天黑的時候路燈自動會亮起來。

□²⁰ **available** [əˋveləbl] (a.) 可取得的

The cell-phone watch has been invented,
but isn't available on the market yet.
行動電話手錶已經發明了，但是在市面上還無法買
到。

| artificial | astounding | automatically | available |

◆□²¹ **awkward** [ˋɔkwəd] (a.) 尷尬的

It was awkward seeing my ex-boyfriend with his new girlfriend.
撞見我的前男友與他的新女友時真是尷尬。

□²² **beloved** [bɪˋlʌvɪd] (a.) 受人喜愛的

The Little Prince is one of the world's most beloved children's books.
《小王子》是世界上最受喜愛的童話書之一。

◆□²³ **bewildering** [bɪˋwɪldərɪŋ] (a.) 令人困惑的

There are a bewildering number of desserts to choose from at this restaurant.
這家餐廳的甜點多得令人難以選擇。

◆□²⁴ **bizarre** [bɪˋzɑr] (a.) 怪異的

I had a bizarre experience this morning on the way to school.
我今早上學途中有一個奇遇。

awkward　beloved　bewildering　bizarre

N O P Q R S T U V W X Y Z

□²⁵ **bold** [bold] (a.) 大膽的

The company made the bold move of cutting prices 50%.
這家公司做出降價百分之五十的大膽舉動。

□²⁶ **brilliant** [ˈbrɪljənt] (a.) 聰穎的；燦爛的

Einstein was one of the most brilliant scientists ever.
愛因斯坦是有史以來最聰明的科學家之一。

□²⁷ **carefree** [ˈkɛr͵fri] (a.) 無憂無慮的

You can tell from his smile that he's still a carefree student.
從他的微笑可以看出他還是個無憂無慮的學生。

□²⁸ **caring** [ˈkɛrɪŋ] (a.) 關心別人的

My mom is one of the most caring people I know.
我的母親是我所知最關心別人的人之一。

| bold | brilliant | carefree | caring |

□²⁹ **cautious** [ˈkɔʃəs] (a.) 謹慎的，小心的

Be very cautious when traveling alone in Egypt.
在埃及獨自旅遊要十分小心。

□³⁰ **chain** [tʃen] (a.) 連鎖的

McDonald's is the world's largest chain restaurant.
麥當勞是世界最大的連鎖餐廳。

□³¹ **challenging** [ˈtʃælɪndʒɪŋ] (a.) 有挑戰性的

This is the most challenging assignment I've ever received.
這是我所接受過最有挑戰性的任務。

□³² **chilling** [ˈtʃɪlɪŋ] (a.) 可怕的

Visiting the prison was a chilling experience.
參觀監獄是很可怕的經驗。

N O P Q R S T U V W X Y Z

| cautious | chain | challenging | chilling |

A
B
C
D
E
F
G
H
I
J
K
L
M

◆ □³³ **compelling** [kəm`pɛlɪŋ] (a.) 令人無法抵抗的
The lawyer presented compelling evidence for his case.
這名律師為他的案子提出強而有力的證據。

□³⁴ **concerned** [kən`sɜnd] (a.) 憂慮的，擔心的
I'm very concerned about your behavior.
我十分擔心你的行為。

□³⁵ **concise** [kən`saɪs] (a.) 簡潔的
Good writing is always concise
好的文章一定是簡潔的。

□³⁶ **confidential** [ˌkɑnfə`dɛnʃəl] (a.) 機密的
The information discussed in today's office meeting is confidential.
今天公司會議討論的消息是機密的。

compelling   concerned   concise   confidential

◆ □³⁷ **consecutive** [kən`sɛkjətɪv] (a.) 連續的

That team won the championship game four consecutive years.

那支隊伍連續四年贏得錦標賽。

□³⁸ **controversial** [ˌkɑntrə`vɝʃəl] (a.) 引起爭議的

This is one of the most controversial books of the year.

這是今年最受爭議的著作之一。

□³⁹ **corrupt** [kə`rʌpt] (a.) 腐敗的，貪污的

There are corrupt officials in every government.

每個政府都有腐敗的官員。

□⁴⁰ **countless** [`kaʊntlɪs] (a.) 數不清的，無數的

I've spent countless hours trying to figure out this problem.

我已花了無數小時試圖解決這個問題。

N
O
P
Q
R
S
T
U
V
W
X
Y
Z

consecutive | controversial | corrupt | countless

◆□⁴¹ **crude** [krud] (a.) 粗魯的，無禮的

I thought that joke was really crude.
我認為那個玩笑非常不禮貌。

□⁴² **cultural** [ˋkʌltʃərəl] (a.) 文化的

I hope to attend a lot of cultural activities during my stay in New York.
在紐約停留期間，我希望參加許多文化活動。

□⁴³ **curious** [ˋkjʊrɪəs] (a.) 好奇的

Little children are curious about everything they see.
小孩子看到什麼都很好奇。

□⁴⁴ **curly** [ˋkɝlɪ] (a.) 捲髮的；捲曲的

Johnny keeps asking "Why is curly hair curly?"
強尼一直問著：「為什麼捲髮會捲捲的呢？」。

| crude | cultural | curious | curly |

□⁴⁵ **current** [ˋkɝənt] (a.) 目前的

This is my current address, but I'm going to move again next month.
這是我目前的地址，但是我下個月又要搬家了。

□⁴⁶ **currently** [ˋkɝəntlɪ] (adv.) 目前

There are currently two job openings in our company.
我們公司目前有兩個職務空缺。

◆□⁴⁷ **deceitful** [dɪˋsitfəl] (a.) 好欺詐的

That salesman is one of the most deceitful men I've ever known.
我所認識的人中，那個業務員是最會騙人的。

□⁴⁸ **definitely** [ˋdɛfənɪtlɪ] (adv.) 絕對地

If you want to borrow money, the answer is definitely "No."
如果你要借錢，答案是絕對「不行」。

| current | currently | deceitful | definitely |

D

□⁴⁹ **demanding** [dɪˋmændɪŋ] (a.) 要求嚴格的

Interpretation is a very demanding job.
翻譯是一項要求非常嚴格的工作。

□⁵⁰ **densely** [ˋdɛnslɪ] (adv.) 稠密地

My family lives in a densely-populated part of the city.
我的家人住在城裡一個人口稠密的區域。

□⁵¹ **desperate** [ˋdɛspərɪt] (a.) 迫切的

Having lived alone for ten years, she's desperate for some companionship!
獨居十年後，她迫切希望有人作伴。

□⁵² **devoted** [dɪˋvotɪd] (a.) 熱愛的；忠實的

She is really devoted to improving her English.
她非常熱中於加強她的英文。

| demanding | densely | desperate | devoted |

☐⁵³ **disgusting** [dɪsˋgʌstɪŋ] (a.) 令人厭惡的

The way you eat is disgusting.
你的吃相令人厭惡。

☐⁵⁴ **distinct** [dɪˋstɪŋkt] (a.) 清楚的

She has a distinct scar on her cheek.
她的臉頰上有個明顯的疤痕。

☐⁵⁵ **distinctive** [dɪˋstɪŋktɪv] (a.) 獨特的

He's got a very distinctive voice.
他有著非常獨特的嗓音。

☐⁵⁶ **dramatically** [drəˋmætɪk]ɪ] (adv.) 大幅地

The Green Revolution dramatically
increased crop yield.
綠色革命大幅提高了農作物產量。

N
O
P
Q
R
S
T
U
V
W
X
Y
Z

disgusting　distinct　distinctive　dramatically

A
B
C

D E

F
G
H
I
J
K
L
M

□⁵⁷ **dual** [ˈdjuəl] (a.) 雙重的

Jim Carrey often plays characters with dual personalities.
金凱瑞常常扮演雙重人格的角色。

□⁵⁸ **dull** [dʌl] (a.) 枯燥的，呆板的

This class is really dull. Let's leave.
這堂課真的很枯燥，我們走吧。

□⁵⁹ **eager** [ˈigɚ] (a.) 熱切的

Minn is always eager to try new things.
小敏總是熱切地想嘗試新事物。

□⁶⁰ **easygoing** [ˈizɪˌgoɪŋ] (a.) 隨和的

My boss is a very easygoing person.
我的老闆是個很隨和的人。

| dual | dull | eager | easygoing |

□⁶¹ **effective** [əˋfɛktɪv] (a.) 有效的

There's no effective cure for the AIDS virus.
目前並無治癒愛滋病毒的有效療法。

□⁶² **efficient** [əˋfɪʃənt] (a.) 有效率的

The city's transport system is one of the most efficient in Europe.
這城市的交通運輸系統是歐洲最有效率的一個。

□⁶³ **electronic** [ɪ,lɛkˋtrɑnɪk] (a.) 電子的

I gave my sister an electronic dictionary for her birthday.
我送給妹妹電子字典作為她的生日禮物。

□⁶⁴ **elegant** [ˋɛləgənt] (a.) 優雅的，精緻的

Everyone at the ball was dressed in elegant evening wear.
舞會裡的每個人都穿著優雅的晚禮服。

N
O
P
Q
R
S
T
U
V
W
X
Y
Z

| effective | efficient | electronic | elegant |

□⁶⁵ **enormous** [ɪˋnɔrməs] (a.) 龐大的

Pablo Picasso has had enormous influence over modern artists.
畢卡索對現代藝術家產生極大的影響。

◆□⁶⁶ **enterprising** [ˋɛntəˏpraɪzɪŋ] (a.) 有進取心的

Steve is really enterprising. He started his own company when he was 23 years old.
史提夫非常積極進取。他在二十三歲時就成立了自己的公司。

□⁶⁷ **enthusiastic** [ɪnˏθjuzɪˋæstɪk] (a.) 熱中的

He's one of the most enthusiastic students in my class.
他是我班上最熱中的學生之一。

□⁶⁸ **essential** [əˋsɛnʃəl] (a.) 必要的；基本的

A raincoat is an essential piece of hiking equipment.
雨衣是健行的一項基本裝備。

◆ □⁶⁹ **evasive** [ɪˋvesɪv] (a.) 躲避的，逃避的

If you ask him too many personal questions, he becomes very evasive.

如果你問太多私人問題，他會開始逃避。

□⁷⁰ **eventually** [ɪˋvɛntʃʊəlɪ] (adv.) 最後，終於

If you don't get more sleep, you will eventually fall sick.

如果你不睡多一點，最後一定會生病。

□⁷¹ **exactly** [ɪgˋzæktlɪ] (adv.) 完全地

You look exactly like a high-school classmate of mine.

你看起來和我的一位高中同學完全一樣。

◆ □⁷² **exclusive** [ɪkˋsklusɪv] (a.) 獨家的

The magazine published an exclusive interview with the President.

這本雜誌刊載了總統的獨家專訪。

| evasive | eventually | exactly | exclusive |

□⁷³ **exhausting** [ɪɡˋzɔstɪŋ] (a.) 使人筋疲力盡的

Talking to you is exhausting. You're way too formal.
和你說話累死人，你太正經了。

◆□⁷⁴ **exhilarated** [ɪɡˋzɪləˏretɪd] (a.) 興奮的

I felt exhilarated after our hike in the mountains.
在我們登山之後，我感到非常興奮。

◆□⁷⁵ **explosive** [ɪkˋsplosɪv] (a.) 爆炸性的

There was an explosive report on TV last night about the cigarette industry.
昨晚電視上有關於香菸工業的一則爆炸性報導。

□⁷⁶ **expressive** [ɪkˋsprɛsɪv] (a.) 富於表情的

Joan's face is very expressive. I guess that's why she's an actress.
瓊安臉上的表情非常豐富。我想那是她會去當女演員的原因。

exhausting | exhilarated | explosive | expressive

□⁷⁷ **extraordinary** [ɪk`strɔrdn̩,ɛrɪ] (a.) 非凡的

The kid's extraordinary memory impressed his teachers.
這個小孩非凡的記憶力令老師印象深刻。

□⁷⁸ **faint** [fent] (a.) 微弱的

A faint breeze blew through the trees outside my window.
一絲微弱的風吹過我窗外的樹木。

□⁷⁹ **fairly** [`fɛrlɪ] (adv.) 相當地

I have a fairly good idea of where Angela might be hiding.
關於安琪拉的藏身之地，我相當有把握。

□⁸⁰ **fashionable** [`fæʃənəbl] (a.) 流行的

My sister always wears the newest, most fashionable clothes.
我妹妹總是穿著最新穎、最流行的衣服。

N O P Q R S T U V W X Y Z

extraordinary　　faint　　fairly　　fashionable

「字」我挑戰 1

解答請見 p. 290

_____ 1. This is one of the most _____ inventory systems in the world.
(A) anxious
(B) carefree
(C) advanced
(D) corrupt

_____ 2. What project is your division _____ working on?
(A) currently
(B) dramatically
(C) densely
(D) fairly

_____ 3. Since Ted is so _____, everyone gets along with him.
(A) disgusting
(B) enormous
(C) aggressive
(D) easygoing

_____ 4. _____ tourists visit Disneyland every year.
(A) Evasive
(B) Countless
(C) Alternative
(D) Distinctive

_____ 5. Debussy's music is both _____ and
inspiring.
(A) cautious
(B) addicted
(C) appropriate
(D) expressive

_____ 6. Aren't you even a little bit _____ about
what I bought you for your birthday?
(A) curious
(B) enterprising
(C) bizarre
(D) desperate

_____ 7. Linda's _____ attitude makes her very
popular with the boss.
(A) enthusiastic
(B) alarming
(C) artificial
(D) chilling

_____ 8. Few politicians would give a clear opinion
about the _____ topic.
(A) adorable
(B) concise
(C) controversial
(D) exclusive

_____ 9. It's _____ that we finish as quickly as possible.
(A) explosive
(B) essential
(C) crude
(D) abandoned

_____10. I don't think that brand of cereal is _____ in my area.
(A) available
(B) compelling
(C) eager
(D) effective

_____11. My son told me this style of watch is _____ these days.
(A) anonymous
(B) definitely
(C) devoted
(D) fashionable

_____12. You know, that is _____ what I was thinking!
(A) eventually
(B) automatically
(C) exactly
(D) concerned

TIME
Basic Words 888

形容詞／副詞

Chapter 2
81~160

共
240
字

- □ fast-paced 節奏快的，步調快的
- □ fearful 害怕的
- □ feminine 適合婦女的；溫柔的
- □ fierce 激烈的；凶猛的
- □ fit 體能好的
- □ flawed 有缺陷的
- □ full-scale 全面的；照原尺寸的
- □ furious 狂怒的，大發雷霆的
- ■ gifted 有天份的
- □ glamorous 迷人的，富有魅力的
- □ global 全球的
- □ gorgeous 可愛的
- □ grand 盛大的；偉大的
- □ greasy 油膩的
- □ grueling 累人的
- ■ handheld 手持的
- □ harsh 嚴苛的
- □ high-tech 高科技的
- □ horrible 恐怖的
- □ humble 卑微的；謙虛的
- ■ ideal 理想的
- □ identical 完全相同的
- □ illegal 非法的
- □ imaginable 想像得到的
- □ imaginary 想像的
- □ immense 無限的，龐大的
- □ immigrant 移民來的，移入的

- □ immortal 不朽的，永恆的
- □ impressive 令人印象深刻的
- □ incredible 非常的；難以置信的
- □ individual 個別的
- □ infinite 無數的；無限的
- □ initial 最初的，開始的
- □ injured 受傷的
- □ innovative 革新的，創新的
- □ insensitive 感覺遲鈍的
- □ inspirational 鼓舞的
- □ instant 立即的
- □ intense 激烈的，強烈的
- □ interactive 互動的
- □ interior 室內的，內部的
- □ invaluable 無價的，非常珍貴的
- □ invincible 無敵的
- □ irregular 不規則的
- □ irresistible 不能抗拒的
- □ irritable 急躁的，易怒的
- □ isolated 孤立的
- ■ jealous 嫉妒的，吃醋的
- ■ keen 敏銳的
- ■ latest 最新的
- □ limited 有限的
- □ live 現場地
- □ lively 熱鬧的，活潑的
- □ local 當地的

□ located 座落於，位於

□ lone 單獨的

□ loyal 忠誠的

■ magnetic 有磁性的

□ mean 凶惡的

□ memorable 值得懷念的，
難忘的

□ mental 心理的，精神的

□ metaphorical 隱喻的，比喻的

□ military 軍事的

□ miserable 痛苦的，不幸的

□ moral 道德的

□ multi-million 數百萬的

□ multinational 多國的

□ muscular 肌肉發達的

■ nasty 令人討厭的

□ naughty 頑皮的

□ nauseous 想吐的，反胃的

□ negative 負面的

□ nutritional 營養上的

□ nutritious 有營養的

■ obscene 猥褻的，淫亂的

□ odd 古怪的

□ offensive 攻擊性的；無禮的

□ old-fashioned 舊式的，
老式的

□ optimistic 樂觀的

□ original 原創的，本來的

A
B
C
D
E
F
G
H
I
J
K
L
M

□[81] **fast-paced** [`fæst,pest] (a.) 節奏快的，步調快的

Life in Hong Kong is too fast-paced for me.
對我而言，香港生活的節奏太快了。

□[82] **fearful** [`fɪrfəl] (a.) 害怕的

Fearful of defeat, the candidate spent millions of dollars on his campaign.
這位候選人因為害怕失敗，花了數百萬元來競選。

□[83] **feminine** [`fɛmənɪn] (a.) 適合婦女的；溫柔的

This year the fashion is for long dresses in feminine flower-prints.
今年流行嬌柔的印花長洋裝。

◆□[84] **fierce** [fɪrs] (a.) 激烈的；凶猛的

There is going to be fierce competition at this year's Olympic long jump.
今年的奧運跳遠項目將有激烈的競爭。

| fast-paced | fearful | feminine | fierce |

□ 85 **fit** [fɪt] (a.) 體能好的

You can stay fit by doing a lot of exercise.
你多運動，就能維持好體能。

□ 86 **flawed** [flɔd] (a.) 有缺陷的

This business plan is flawed. We need to rethink it.
這項交易計畫有瑕疵，我們必須重新考慮。

□ 87 **full-scale** [ˋful‚skel] (a.) 全面的；照原尺寸的

The UN sent in troops to prevent full-scale war.
聯合國派兵進駐，以防爆發全面戰爭。

◆ □ 88 **furious** [ˋfjʊrɪəs] (a.) 狂怒的，大發雷霆的

Alice was furious when she found out about the broken vase.
愛麗絲發現破花瓶之後大發雷霆。

N O P Q R S T U V W X Y Z

| fit | flawed | full-scale | furious |

A
B
C
D
E
F

G
H

I
J
K
L
M

□⁸⁹ **gifted** [ˋgɪftɪd] (a.) 有天份的

She is a gifted musician, but she cannot read music.
她是一名有天份的音樂家，但她不會讀譜。

◆□⁹⁰ **glamorous** [ˋglæmərəs] (a.) 迷人的，富有魅力的

Many think that being a reporter is a glamorous job.
許多人認為當記者是一份迷人的工作。

□⁹¹ **global** [ˋglobl] (a.) 全球的

Everyone says the earth is becoming a global village.
人人都說世界逐漸成為一個地球村。

◆□⁹² **gorgeous** [ˋgɔrdʒəs] (a.) 非常美的，美極了

The girl sitting next to me on the subway was just gorgeous.
地鐵裡坐在我旁邊的那個女孩真是可愛。

| gifted | glamorous | global | gorgeous |

□⁹³ **grand** [grænd] (a.) 盛大的；偉大的

The grand opening ceremony is very impressive.
盛大的開幕典禮令人印象深刻。

□⁹⁴ **greasy** [ˋgrisɪ] (a.) 油膩的

This dish is too greasy. I can't finish it.
這道菜太油膩了，我吃不完。

◆□⁹⁵ **grueling** [ˋgruəlɪŋ] (a.) 累人的

The military put the young men through five grueling days of training.
軍方讓這些年輕人接受為期五天筋疲力竭的訓練。

□⁹⁶ **handheld** [ˋhænd͵hɛld] (a.) 手持的

My kid brother is really good at handheld video games.
我弟弟很會玩手持機種的電玩遊戲。

N O P Q R S T U V W X Y Z

| grand | greasy | grueling | handheld |

A
B
C
D
E
F
G
H
I
J
K
L
M

◆ □⁹⁷ **harsh** [harʃ] (a.) 嚴苛的

Don't you think your criticism was a little too harsh?
你不覺得你的批評有點太嚴苛嗎？

□⁹⁸ **high-tech** [ˈhaɪˋtɛk] (a.) 高科技的

A high-tech revolution is changing the way people shop.
一場高科技革命正在改變人們購物的方式。

□⁹⁹ **horrible** [ˈhɔrəbḷ] (a.) 恐怖的

I had a horrible dream last night.
我昨晚做了一個恐怖的夢。

□¹⁰⁰ **humble** [ˈhʌmbḷ] (a.) 卑微的；謙虛的

Many millionaires came from humble beginnings.
許多百萬富翁都出身卑微。

| harsh | high-tech | horrible | humble |

□ 101 **ideal** [aɪˋdɪəl] (a.) 理想的

This is really the ideal location to build a house.
這真是蓋房子的理想地點。

□ 102 **identical** [aɪˋdɛntɪkl] (a.) 完全相同的

That shirt is identical to the one you were wearing yesterday!
這件襯衫和你昨天穿的那件完全相同！

□ 103 **illegal** [ɪˋligl] (a.) 非法的

It's illegal to gamble in Taiwan.
在台灣，賭博是非法的。

□ 104 **imaginable** [ɪˋmædʒɪnəbl] (a.) 想像得到的

This is the best present imaginable.
這是我所能想到最好的禮物了。

N
O
P
Q
R
S
T
U
V
W
X
Y
Z

| ideal | identical | illegal | imaginable |

A
B
C
D
E
F
G
H
I
J
K
L
M

□ [105] **imaginary** [ɪˋmædʒə͵nɛrɪ] (a.) 想像的

Children have an imaginary world of their own.
兒童有他們自己想像的世界。

□ [106] **immense** [ɪˋmɛns] (a.) 無限的，龐大的

The Sahara Desert is an immense area of sand.
撒哈拉沙漠是片廣大的沙地。

□ [107] **immigrant** [ˋɪməgrənt] (a.) 移民來的，移入的

The Asian-American grew up in an immigrant family.
這名亞裔美國人在移民家庭長大。

□ [108] **immortal** [ɪˋmɔrtl] (a.) 不朽的，永恆的

Shakespeare is immortal because of the works he left behind.
莎士比亞因為遺留下來的作品而不朽。

| imaginary | immense | immigrant | immortal |

□ 109 **impressive** [ɪmˋprɛsɪv] (a.) 令人印象深刻的

Richard gave an impressive speech at the wedding.
理查在婚禮上的演講令人印象深刻。

□ 110 **incredible** [ɪnˋkrɛdəbl] (a.) 非常的；難以置信的

The manager deals with an incredible amount of stress every day.
經理每天要面臨非常大的壓力。

□ 111 **individual** [ˌɪndəˋvɪdʒʊəl] (a.) 個別的

We can design a house to suit your individual needs.
我們可以設計一棟房屋來符合你的個別需求。

□ 112 **infinite** [ˋɪnfənɪt] (a.) 無數的；無限的

There seems to be an infinite number of stars in the sky.
天上似乎有無數的星星。

N
O
P
Q
R
S
T
U
V
W
X
Y
Z

| impressive | incredible | individual | infinite |

□ 113 **initial** [ɪˋnɪʃəl] (a.) 最初的，開始的

After the initial shock wears off, living overseas isn't that difficult.
在最初的衝擊逐漸消失後，在海外生活其實並不那麼困難。

□ 114 **injured** [ˋɪndʒəd] (a.) 受傷的

Don't put too much weight on your injured leg.
你受傷的那條腿不要承受太多重量。

□ 115 **innovative** [ˋɪnə͵vetɪv] (a.) 革新的，創新的

I think Jack's ideas are very innovative.
我認為傑克的點子頗為創新。

□ 116 **insensitive** [ɪnˋsɛnsətɪv] (a.) 感覺遲鈍的

She has a rich husband, but he's really insensitive.
她丈夫很有錢，不過卻很遲鈍。

| initial | injured | innovative | insensitive |

□¹¹⁷ **inspirational** [ˌɪnspəˋreʃənl] (a.) 鼓舞的

Your speech about recycling was very inspirational.
你關於資源回收的演說十分振奮人心。

□¹¹⁸ **instant** [ˋɪnstənt] (a.) 立即的

There is a place around the corner where you can get instant photos taken.
在那轉角有個地方可以拍快照。

□¹¹⁹ **intense** [ɪnˋtɛns] (a.) 激烈的，強烈的

I have an intense pain in my back.
我的背部劇痛。

□¹²⁰ **interactive** [ˌɪntɚˋæktɪv] (a.) 互動的

We played a lot of interactive games that taught us how to communicate better with others. 我們玩許多互動遊戲，這些遊戲教我們如何與其他人溝通得更好。

inspirational　　instant　　intense　　interactive

◆□¹²¹ **interior** [ɪnˋtɪrɪə] (a.) 室內的；內部的

She majored in interior design in college.
她在大學主修的是室內設計。

□¹²² **invaluable** [ɪnˋvæljəbl] (a.) 無價的，非常珍貴的

Your invaluable assistance has made it possible for us to finish this project on time.
你寶貴的援助使我們得以準時完成這項計畫。

◆□¹²³ **invincible** [ɪnˋvɪnsəbl] (a.) 無敵的

After taking the survival course, we felt invincible.
上過求生課程之後，我們覺得自己是無敵的。

□¹²⁴ **irregular** [ɪˋrɛgjələ] (a.) 不規則的

Her health problems are due to her irregular sleeping habits.
她的健康問題是出於不規律的睡眠習慣。

| interior | invaluable | invincible | irregular |

◆ □¹²⁵ **irresistible** [ˌɪrɪˋzɪstəbḷ] (a.) 不能抗拒的

I do anything my girlfriend wants me to do because her smile is irresistible.

我對女友百依百順，因為她的微笑令人無法抗拒。

◆ □¹²⁶ **irritable** [ˋɪrətəbḷ] (a.) 急躁的，易怒的

Mom is always irritable when she has a bad day at work.

母親工作不順利時總是暴躁易怒。

□¹²⁷ **isolated** [ˋaɪsḷˌetɪd] (a.) 孤立的

The isolated island of Tasmania produced some unique animals.

孤立的塔斯馬尼亞島出產一些獨特的動物。

□¹²⁸ **jealous** [ˋdʒɛləs] (a.) 嫉妒的，吃醋的

My boyfriend gets jealous if I talk to other boys.

要是我和其他男孩子說話，我男朋友就會吃醋。

| irresistible | irritable | isolated | jealous |

□¹²⁹ **keen** [kin] (a.) 敏銳的

Dogs have a keen sense of smell.
狗有敏銳的嗅覺。

□¹³⁰ **latest** [ˋletɪst] (a.) 最新的

Internet news can be updated every hour, to
keep the audience informed of the latest
events. 網路新聞可以每小時更新，讓觀眾知道最
新的事件。

□¹³¹ **limited** [ˋlɪmɪtɪd] (a.) 有限的

There were a limited number of free seats
available for the movie.
這場電影有提供限量的免費座位。

□¹³² **live** [laɪv] (adv.) 現場地

The rock concert will be broadcasted live on
MTV.
這場搖滾演唱會將在 MTV 頻道上現場實況轉播。

| keen | latest | limited | live |

□ 133 **lively** [ˋlaɪvlɪ] (a.) 熱鬧的，活潑的

I watched a lively discussion about tax issues on TV last night.
昨晚我看了一場關於稅務議題熱鬧的電視辯論。

□ 134 **local** [ˋlokḷ] (a.) 當地的

Make sure to try the local foods when you travel to Italy!
當你去義大利旅行，一定要試試當地的食物！

□ 135 **located** [ˋloketɪd] (a.) 座落於，位於

Our new office is located on Tun-hua South Road.
我們的新辦公室位於敦化南路。

□ 136 **lone** [lon] (a.) 單獨的

There was a lone hawk flying above my house yesterday.
有隻孤鷹昨天在我家房子上方飛翔。

| lively | local | located | lone |

□¹³⁷ **loyal** [ˈlɔɪəl] (a.) 忠誠的

John isn't very smart, but he's one of the
most loyal people I know.
約翰不是很精明，卻是我所認識最忠誠的人之一。

◆□¹³⁸ **magnetic** [mægˋnɛtɪk] (a.) 有磁性的

Every credit card has a magnetic strip.
每張信用卡都有磁條。

□¹³⁹ **mean** [min] (a.) 凶惡的

That mean old man yells and complains
because he's lonely.
那個凶惡的老人因為寂寞而吼叫抱怨。

□¹⁴⁰ **memorable** [ˈmɛmərəbl] (a.) 值得懷念的，難忘的

My wedding day was the most memorable
day of my life.
我的婚禮是我這輩子最難忘的一天。

| loyal | magnetic | mean | memorable |

□ 141 **mental** [ˋmɛntl] (a.) 心理的，精神的

This is a hospital for mental illness.
這是一家精神病院。

◆ □ 142 **metaphorical** [ˌmɛtəˋfɔrɪkl] (a.) 隱喻的，比喻的

His third novel is written in a very
metaphorical style.
他第三本小說是用非常隱喻的手法寫的。

□ 143 **military** [ˋmɪləˌtɛrɪ] (a.) 軍事的

Taiwan's military spending is increasing
every year.
台灣的軍事支出逐年增加。

□ 144 **miserable** [ˋmɪzərəbl] (a.) 痛苦的，不幸的

I'm always miserable in the summertime
because I can't take the heat.
因為我很怕熱，所以夏天總是十分痛苦。

| mental | metaphorical | military | miserable |

A
B
C
D
E
F
G
H
I
J
K
L
M

□ [145] **moral** [ˋmɔrəl] (a.) 道德的

There is a moral lesson to this story.
這個故事有個道德寓意。

□ [146] **multi-million** [ˌmʌltəˋmɪljən] (a.) 數百萬的

The company conducted a multi-million
dollar research project.
這家公司進行一項數百萬元的研究計畫。

□ [147] **multinational** [ˋmʌltɪˋnæʃənl] (a.) 多國的

Our school tries to maintain a multinational
student body.
我們學校嘗試維持多國學生的結構。

◆□ [148] **muscular** [ˋmʌskjələ] (a.) 肌肉發達的

I don't find muscular men very attractive.
我不覺得肌肉發達的男人有吸引力。

| moral | multi-million | multinational | muscular |

◆□¹⁴⁹ **nasty** [ˋnæstɪ] (a.) 令人討厭的

I got a nasty letter from the phone company today that says we need to pay our phone bill. 我今天收到電信公司討厭的來函，要我們付帳單。

◆□¹⁵⁰ **naughty** [ˋnɔtɪ] (a.) 頑皮的

I was a naughty boy when I was growing up. 我在成長時是個淘氣的男孩。

◆□¹⁵¹ **nauseous** [ˋnɔʃəs] (a.) 想吐的，反胃的

I felt nauseous after the roller-coaster ride. 我坐了雲霄飛車後覺得想吐。

□¹⁵² **negative** [ˋnɛgətɪv] (a.) 負面的

There is a positive and a negative way of looking at everything. 看任何事都有正面與負面的看法。

N
O
P
Q
R
S
T
U
V
W
X
Y
Z

| nasty | naughty | nauseous | negative |

A
B
C
D
E
F
G
H
I
J
K
L
M

□ ¹⁵³ **nutritional** [njuˋtrɪʃənl] (a.) 營養上的

It's important to know the nutritional value of the foods you eat.
知道你所吃的食物的營養價值十分重要。

◆ □ ¹⁵⁴ **nutritious** [njuˋtrɪʃəs] (a.) 有營養的

I eat an extremely nutritious diet, so I seldom get sick.
我的飲食非常有營養，因此我很少生病。

◆ □ ¹⁵⁵ **obscene** [əbˋsin] (a.) 猥褻的，淫亂的

I have been receiving obscene phone calls for the last few weeks.
過去幾個星期以來我一直接到猥褻的電話。

□ ¹⁵⁶ **odd** [ɑd] (a.) 古怪的

I think my neighbor Mr. Jones is a little odd.
我覺得我的鄰居瓊斯先生有點古怪。

| nutritional | nutritious | obscene | odd |

□157 **offensive** [əˋfɛnsɪv] (a.) 攻擊性的；無禮的

Do you think this ad is offensive?
你認為這支廣告有攻擊性嗎？

□158 **old-fashioned** [ˋoldˋfæʃənd] (a.) 舊式的，老式的

Pagers are now considered old-fashioned technology.
呼叫器現在被認為是舊式的科技。

□159 **optimistic** [ˌɑptəˋmɪstɪk] (a.) 樂觀的

After getting his college degree, John was optimistic about finding a job he liked.
拿到大學學位後，約翰對找到喜歡的工作感到樂觀。

□160 **original** [əˋrɪdʒənl] (a.) 原創的，本來的

That is one of the most original paintings I have ever seen.
那是我所見過最有原創性的畫作之一。

N
O

P
Q
R
S
T
U
V
W
X
Y
Z

「字」我挑戰 2

解答請見 p. 290

_____ 1. Unfortunately, many of us receive pornographic and _____ e-mails regularly.
(A) immortal
(B) furious
(C) obscene
(D) keen

_____ 2. The _____ actress wore a beautiful gown to the party.
(A) multi-million
(B) instant
(C) imaginable
(D) gorgeous

_____ 3. Even though things aren't going well right now, try to stay _____ about the future.
(A) identical
(B) optimistic
(C) fearful
(D) irritable

_____ 4. The student felt _____ after he failed his test.
(A) miserable
(B) grand
(C) impressive
(D) invincible

_____ 5. Fast food restaurants rarely have anything
_____ on the menu.
(A) interactive
(B) greasy
(C) immigrant
(D) nutritious

_____ 6. To the end, the soldiers were _____ to
their commander.
(A) original
(B) loyal
(C) feminine
(D) injured

_____ 7. After winning the football championship,
the star player was _____ , giving credit
to his teammates.
(A) humble
(B) innovative
(C) jealous
(D) isolated

_____ 8. The teacher told the _____ student to
stay in his seat.
(A) grueling
(B) imaginary
(C) inspirational
(D) naughty

_____ 9. This market gets very _____ in the late afternoon.
(A) offensive
(B) lively
(C) irresistible
(D) lone

_____ 10. Coca Cola, a _____ corporation, has offices around the world.
(A) military
(B) multinational
(C) memorable
(D) latest

_____ 11. Although the dog was small, it was still very _____ .
(A) flawed
(B) ideal
(C) individual
(D) fierce

_____ 12. _____ computers are becoming more powerful every year.
(A) Insensitive
(B) Isolated
(C) Handheld
(D) Old-fashioned

TIME
Basic Words 888

形容詞／副詞

共 **240** 字

Chapter 3

161~240

□ originally 原來，本來
□ outspoken 坦率直言的
□ overall 全部的，整體的
□ overweight 過重的
■ patient 有耐心的
□ petty 小氣的；瑣碎的
□ physical 身體的，肉體的
□ physically 身體上
□ precious 寶貴的
□ prestigious 有名望的
□ previous 先前的
□ primitive 原始的
□ prized 受珍視的
□ professional 職業的；專業的
□ profitable 有利潤的
□ profound 深刻的
□ prominent 突起的
□ proper 恰當的，正確的
■ radical 激進的
□ radically 完全地，根本地
□ rebellious 叛逆的
□ reckless 魯莽的，不顧後果的
□ recognized 公認的；
　　被人認識的
□ regular 一般的，普通的
□ reluctant 不情願的
□ remote 遙遠的；遙控的
□ reusable 可重複使用的

□ revolting 可憎的，令人厭惡的
□ ridiculous 可笑的，荒謬的
□ righteous 正直的，守法的
□ ripe（果實、穀物）成熟的
□ risky 冒險的
□ rural 鄉村的
■ sacred 神聖的
□ seasonal 季節性的
□ severe 猛烈的；嚴重的
□ shifting 不斷變化的
□ silly 愚蠢的
□ similar 類似的，相似的
□ skinny 瘦的，皮包骨的
□ solemn 嚴肅的
□ spare 多餘的
□ spicy 辣的
□ stressful 充滿壓力的
□ strict 嚴格的
□ stunning 驚人的
□ suitable 適合的
□ superb 一流的，極好的
□ supposedly 據說，據稱
□ supreme 最高的
□ swift 快速的
■ talented 有才華的
□ technical 技術的
□ temporary 暫時的
□ thrilling 刺激的，驚悚的

□ tough　艱苦的

□ tragic　悲劇的

□ trendy　流行的

□ tricky　需技巧的；棘手的

□ trivial　瑣碎的

□ trustworthy　值得信賴的

■ ultimate　終極的；理想的

□ unarmed　無武裝的

□ unbeatable　打不垮的，無敵的

□ undisputed　毫無疑問的

□ unfortunately　不幸地

□ unhealthy　不健康的

□ unique　獨一無二的

□ unlikely　不太可能的

□ unlimited　無限制的

□ unnecessary　沒必要的

□ unwilling　不願意的

□ upset　沮喪的

■ vague　模糊的

□ various　各式各樣的

□ versatile　多功能的；
　　多才多藝的

□ violent　暴力的

□ virtually　幾乎；事實上

□ vulnerable　脆弱的；
　　易受攻擊的

■ widespread　廣泛的，普及的

A
B
C
D
E
F
G
H
I
J
K
L
M

☐ 161 **originally** [əˋrɪdʒən̩lɪ] (adv.) 原來，本來

We had originally planned to go to Paris, but ended up going to Rome.
我們原先計劃前往巴黎，結果卻去了羅馬。

◆ ☐ 162 **outspoken** [ˋautˋspokən] (a.) 坦率直言的

Your outspoken ways are going to get you in trouble.
你坦率直言的態度會替你惹上麻煩。

☐ 163 **overall** [ˋovɚ͵ɔl] (a.) 全部的，整體的

I got an overall score of 98% on the final exams.
我的期末考總成績是九十八分。

☐ 164 **overweight** [ˋovɚ͵wet] (a.) 過重的

Being overweight can cause a lot of health problems.
體重過重會導致許多健康上的問題。

□ [165] **patient** [ˈpeʃənt] (a.) 有耐心的

Patient teachers are hard to find.
有耐心的老師難尋。

◆□ [166] **petty** [ˈpɛtɪ] (a.) 小氣的；瑣碎的

It's very petty to argue over a few dollars.
為了幾塊錢而爭執真是太小氣了。

□ [167] **physical** [ˈfɪzɪkl̩] (a.) 身體的，肉體的

You may increase your physical strength by lifting weights a few times a week.
你可以藉著一星期舉重幾次，增強體力。

□ [168] **physically** [ˈfɪzɪkl̩ɪ] (adv.) 身體上

Physically I find her very attractive, but we don't have the same outlook on life.
就身體而言我覺得她很有魅力，但我們的人生觀不同。

| patient | petty | physical | physically |

□ 169 **precious** [ˋprɛʃəs] (a.) 寶貴的

My health is my most precious possession.
我的健康是我最寶貴的財產。

◆ □ 170 **prestigious** [prɛsˋtɪdʒɪəs] (a.) 有名望的

Tom graduated from a prestigious school
but ended up working at McDonald's !
湯姆畢業於名校，最後卻在麥當勞工作！

□ 171 **previous** [ˋprivɪəs] (a.) 先前的

This English teacher is much better than the
previous one.
這個英文老師比先前的那個好多了。

◆ □ 172 **primitive** [ˋprɪmətɪv] (a.) 原始的

Biting is a very primitive way for a child to
express his anger.
咬人是小孩表現憤怒的一種原始方式。

| precious | prestigious | previous | primitive |

□ 173 **prized** [praɪzd] (a.) 受珍視的

Barbie is the girl's most prized possession.
芭比娃娃是這個女孩最珍貴的家當。

□ 174 **professional** [prəˋfɛʃənl] (a.) 職業的；專業的

My goal is to become a professional athlete.
我的目標是成為職業運動員。

□ 175 **profitable** [ˋprɑfɪtəbl] (a.) 有利潤的

He runs a profitable business selling
second-hand books to students.
他賣二手書給學生，是個頗有利潤的生意。

□ 176 **profound** [prəˋfaʊnd] (a.) 深刻的

That book is funny, but it's not very
profound.
那本書有趣，但不是很有深度。

N O **P** Q R S T U V W X Y Z

| prized | professional | profitable | profound |

♦ □177 **prominent** [ˋprɑmənənt] (a.) 突起的

Barbara Streissand has a prominent nose.
芭芭拉史翠珊有個大鼻子。

□178 **proper** [ˋprɑpɚ] (a.) 恰當的，正確的

We're going to an expensive restaurant—those sandals aren't proper.
我們要去一家昂貴的餐廳──穿那雙涼鞋並不恰當。

□179 **radical** [ˋrædɪk!] (a.) 激進的

I think his ideas are really radical.
我認為他的想法非常激進。

□180 **radically** [ˋrædɪk!ɪ] (adv.) 完全地，根本地

Bess and Karen have radically different beliefs about religion.
貝絲與凱倫對於宗教有完全不同的信仰。

| prominent | proper | radical | radically |

□ ¹⁸¹ **rebellious** [rɪˋbɛljəs] (a.) 叛逆的

Our son is going through a rebellious stage right now.
我們兒子現在正在歷經叛逆期。

♦ □ ¹⁸² **reckless** [ˋrɛklɪs] (a.) 魯莽的，不顧後果的

He was fined $6,000 for reckless driving.
他因為魯莽駕駛被罰款六千元。

□ ¹⁸³ **recognized** [ˋrɛkəg͵naɪzd] (a.) 公認的；被人認識的

Tom Cruise is recognized as one of Hollywood's biggest stars.
湯姆克魯斯被公認為好萊塢的巨星之一。

□ ¹⁸⁴ **regular** [ˋrɛgjələ] (a.) 一般的，普通的

I'm just a regular guy.
我只是個很普通的人。

N
O
P
Q
R
S
T
U
V
W
X
Y
Z

◆□¹⁸⁵ **reluctant** [rɪˋlʌktənt] (a.) 不情願的

The boy was most reluctant to part with his dog when he had to go back to school.
這個男孩必須回學校去的時候，非常不願與他的狗分離。

□¹⁸⁶ **remote** [rɪˋmot] (a.) 遙遠的；遙控的

It's my dream to visit the remote areas of China.
探訪中國偏遠地區是我的夢想。

□¹⁸⁷ **reusable** [riˋjuzəbl] (a.) 可重複使用的

Plastic garbage bags are not reusable.
塑膠垃圾袋無法重複使用。

◆□¹⁸⁸ **revolting** [rɪˋvoltɪŋ] (a.) 可憎的，令人厭惡的

I am never eating in this restaurant again; the food was revolting.
我不會再來這家餐廳用餐了，他們的食物令人噁心。

| reluctant | remote | reusable | revolting |

□ 189 **ridiculous** [rɪˋdɪkjələs] (a.) 可笑的，荒謬的

He looks ridiculous in that old hat.
他戴那頂舊帽子很好笑。

◆ □ 190 **righteous** [ˋraɪtʃəs] (a.) 正直的，守法的

He is regarded as a righteous man.
他被認為是個正直的人。

□ 191 **ripe** [raɪp] (a.)（果實、穀物）成熟的

Fields of ripe wheat were ready for harvesting.
田裡成熟的麥子已經可以收割了。

□ 192 **risky** [ˋrɪskɪ] (a.) 冒險的

I don't invest in the stock market because it's too risky.
我不投資股市，因為太冒險了。

| ridiculous | righteous | ripe | risky |

A
B
C
D
E
F
G
H
I
J
K
L
M

◆□¹⁹³ **rural** [ˋrurəl] (a.) 鄉村的

I grew up in a rural environment.
我在鄉村的環境中長大。

◆□¹⁹⁴ **sacred** [ˋsekrɪd] (a.) 神聖的

Churches and temples are both sacred places.
教堂與寺廟都是神聖的地方。

□¹⁹⁵ **seasonal** [ˋsizṇəl] (a.) 季節性的

Seasonal rains bring cooler temperatures.
季節性的降雨使氣溫較涼爽。

□¹⁹⁶ **severe** [səˋvɪr] (a.) 猛烈的；嚴重的

There have been several severe rainstorms in the last week.
上週有幾場猛烈的暴風雨。

| rural | sacred | seasonal | severe |

□ [197] **shifting** [ˈʃɪftɪŋ] (a.) 不斷變化的

Shifting market trends have made many businesses uncomfortable.
不斷變化的市場趨勢已經令許多企業感到不安。

□ [198] **silly** [ˈsɪlɪ] (a.) 愚蠢的

The boss is very busy; don't ask him any silly questions.
老闆相當忙；別問他任何蠢問題。

□ [199] **similar** [ˈsɪmələ] (a.) 類似的，相似的

The twins have similar appearances, but different personalities.
這對雙胞胎面貌相似，個性卻不同。

□ [200] **skinny** [ˈskɪnɪ] (a.) 瘦的，皮包骨的

You really should eat more—you're too skinny.
你真的該多吃點——你太瘦了。

N
O
P
Q
R
S
T
U
V
W
X
Y
Z

| shifting | silly | similar | skinny |

◆ □²⁰¹ **solemn** [ˋsɑləm] (a.) 嚴肅的

The judge looked solemn as he was about to pass sentence.
法官要判刑時看起來很嚴肅。

□²⁰² **spare** [spɛr] (a.) 多餘的

Excuse me, sir. Do you have any spare change?
先生對不起，你有多餘的零錢嗎？

□²⁰³ **spicy** [ˋspaɪsɪ] (a.) 辣的

Korean food is known for being very spicy.
韓國食物以辛辣著稱。

□²⁰⁴ **stressful** [ˋstrɛsfəl] (a.) 充滿壓力的

Working two jobs at once can be very stressful.
身兼二職壓力很大。

☐²⁰⁵ **strict** [strɪkt] (a.) 嚴格的

My parents weren't very strict with me when I was growing up.
我父母在我成長過程中對我並不十分嚴格。

◆☐²⁰⁶ **stunning** [ˈstʌnɪŋ] (a.) 驚人的

That is a stunning dress you are wearing.
你的穿著令人驚艷。

☐²⁰⁷ **suitable** [ˈsutəbl] (a.) 適合的

That dress isn't suitable for the business meeting.
那套衣服不適合這次的業務會議。

◆☐²⁰⁸ **superb** [suˋpɝb] (a.) 一流的，極好的

Your mother's Thanksgiving dinner was superb!
你母親的感恩節大餐真是太棒了！

N
O
P
Q
R
S
T
U
V
W
X
Y
Z

| strict | stunning | suitable | superb |

□²⁰⁹ **supposedly** [sə`pozɪdlɪ] (adv.) 據說，據稱

Tom supposedly has a girlfriend; why did he ask me out?
湯姆據說有女朋友，為什麼他還約我？

◆□²¹⁰ **supreme** [sə`prim] (a.) 最高的

Chiang Kai-shek was the supreme leader of the R.O.C. for many years.
蔣介石擔任中華民國多年的最高領袖。

□²¹¹ **swift** [swɪft] (a.) 快速的

The police took swift action against the squatters.
警察的違建住戶採取了快速的行動。

□²¹² **talented** [`tæləntɪd] (a.) 有才華的

Mira is one of the most talented musicians I know.
米拉是我所知道最有才華的音樂家之一。

□²¹³ **technical** [ˈtɛknɪkl̩] (a.) 技術的

Your question is very technical. I'll have to look up the answer.
你問的是技術性的問題，我得查查答案。

□²¹⁴ **temporary** [ˈtɛmpəˌrɛrɪ] (a.) 暫時的

I apologize for giving you such a small desk. It's only temporary.
很抱歉給你這麼小的一張書桌。這只是暫時的。

◆ □²¹⁵ **thrilling** [ˈθrɪlɪŋ] (a.) 刺激的，驚悚的

Roller coasters may be thrilling for some, but they're terrifying for me.
對有些人而言雲霄飛車可能很刺激，但對我而言很恐怖。

□²¹⁶ **tough** [tʌf] (a.) 艱苦的

My grandfather said that he had a tough time during the Great Depression.
我祖父說他在經濟大蕭條期間的日子很困苦。

A
B
C
D
E
F
G
H
I
J
K
L
M

□²¹⁷ **tragic** [ˈtrædʒɪk] (a.) 悲劇的

His sister died in a tragic car accident.
他的姐姐死於一場悲慘的車禍意外。

◆□²¹⁸ **trendy** [ˈtrɛndɪ] (a.) 流行的

This is a really trendy toy. You should buy one.
這個玩具非常流行。你應該買一個。

◆□²¹⁹ **tricky** [ˈtrɪkɪ] (a.) 需技巧的；棘手的

Fishing on ice is a tricky business.
在冰上釣魚是需要技巧的事。

◆□²²⁰ **trivial** [ˈtrɪvɪəl] (a.) 瑣碎的

Many couples argue over trivial matters.
許多夫妻為了瑣碎的小事爭執。

| tragic | trendy | tricky | trivial |

□²²¹ **trustworthy** [ˈtrʌst͵wɝðɪ] (a.) 值得信賴的

It always takes some time to figure out if someone is trustworthy or not.
一個人是否值得信賴，總是需要一些時間來了解。

◆ □²²² **ultimate** [ˈʌltəmɪt] (a.) 終極的；理想的

My ultimate dream is to be an actor.
我最終的夢想是要當演員。

□²²³ **unarmed** [ʌnˋɑrmd] (a.) 無武裝的

I can't shoot at an unarmed man.
我不能向手無寸鐵的人開槍。

□²²⁴ **unbeatable** [ʌnˋbitəbl] (a.) 打不垮的，無敵的

This basketball team was unbeatable last year.
這支籃球隊去年戰無不勝。

□ 225 **undisputed** [ˌʌndɪˋspjutɪd] (a.) 毫無疑問的

Steven Spielberg is the undisputed king of directors.
史帝芬史匹柏是無庸置疑的導演之王。

□ 226 **unfortunately** [ʌnˋfɔrtʃənɪtlɪ] (adv.) 不幸地

I'd love to go to the party with you.
Unfortunately, I have to work.
我很想跟你一起參加宴會。不幸的是，我必須工作。

□ 227 **unhealthy** [ʌnˋhɛlθɪ] (a.) 不健康的

He leads a terribly unhealthy lifestyle.
他的生活方式極不健康。

□ 228 **unique** [juˋnik] (a.) 獨一無二的

Her eyes are of a unique color: a dark green.
她眼睛的顏色很獨特，是深綠色的。

□ [229] **unlikely** [ʌn`laɪklɪ] (a.) 不太可能的

It is unlikely that they will ever find the killer.
他們不太可能找出兇手。

□ [230] **unlimited** [ʌn`lɪmɪtɪd] (a.) 無限制的

There are an unlimited number of places
you can go on vacation.
有數不清的地方可供你度假。

□ [231] **unnecessary** [ʌn`nɛsə,sɛrɪ] (a.) 沒必要的

It's claimed the police used unnecessary
force to control the crowds at last Saturday's
demonstration. 據說警方使用不必要的武力控制
星期六那天的遊行示威。

□ [232] **unwilling** [ʌn`wɪlɪŋ] (a.) 不願意的

The workers are unwilling to accept a pay
cut.
工人們不願接受減薪。

| unlikely | unlimited | unnecessary | unwilling |

□²³³ **upset** [ʌpˋsɛt] (a.) 沮喪的

The young man is upset because he just broke up with his girlfriend.
這個年輕人很沮喪，因為他剛剛和女朋友分手。

◆□²³⁴ **vague** [veg] (a.) 模糊的

I asked him what he did last night, but his answers were all very vague.
我問他昨晚做了什麼，但他的回答都很含糊。

□²³⁵ **various** [ˋvɛrɪəs] (a.) 各式各樣的

For various reasons, I must go abroad to study.
基於種種的原因，我一定要出國唸書。

◆□²³⁶ **versatile** [ˋvɜsətḷ] (a.) 多功能的；多才多藝的

The new mobile phones are versatile machines.
新的行動電話是多功能的機器。

| upset | vague | various | versatile |

□237 **violent** [`vaɪələnt] (a.) 暴力的

Violent children need extra care and attention.
暴力的兒童需要特別的照料與注意。

□238 **virtually** [`vɝtʃʊəlɪ] (adv.) 幾乎；事實上

Life is found virtually everywhere on earth.
地球上幾乎每一個地方都有生命。

◆□239 **vulnerable** [`vʌlnərəbl̩] (a.) 脆弱的；易受攻擊的

A boxer always looks for his opponent's vulnerable points.
拳擊手總是在找尋對手的弱點。

□240 **widespread** [`waɪd,sprɛd] (a.) 廣泛的，普及的

There is a widespread belief that the Internet will become more and more important.
人們普遍相信網際網路會愈來愈重要。

N
O
P
Q
R
S
T
U
V
W
X
Y
Z

| violent | virtually | vulnerable | widespread |

「字」我挑戰 3

解答請見 p. 290

_____ 1. This book has a lot of _____ ideas in it.
  (A) reusable
  (B) spare
  (C) profound
  (D) various

_____ 2. Try to be _____ with your colleague,
  even though you don't get along.
  (A) patient
  (B) primitive
  (C) stressful
  (D) vague

_____ 3. The number of _____ children is rising
  every year.
  (A) seasonal
  (B) overweight
  (C) trivial
  (D) physical

_____ 4. _____ products are only popular for a
  short period of time.
  (A) Unarmed
  (B) Outspoken
  (C) Recognized
  (D) Trendy

_____ 5. _____, I planned to study economics, but then I decided to study engineering.
(A) Radically
(B) Originally
(C) Supposedly
(D) Physically

_____ 6. Remember to behave in a _____ manner when the guests arrive.
(A) revolting
(B) skinny
(C) technical
(D) proper

_____ 7. The only _____ part of the castle was its front entrance.
(A) vulnerable
(B) rural
(C) tragic
(D) unhealthy

_____ 8. Emily has been a _____ violinist for 15 years.
(A) previous
(B) shifting
(C) widespread
(D) professional

_____ 9. My father is _____ to do business with people he doesn't know well.
(A) similar
(B) reluctant
(C) prestigious
(D) remote

_____10. In some religions, certain animals are _____.
(A) undisputed
(B) sacred
(C) versatile
(D) severe

_____11.Our corporate sales division has been very _____ this year.
(A) suitable
(B) unique
(C) profitable
(D) radical

_____12. The government's response to the natural disaster was _____ and efficient.
(A) swift
(B) ultimate
(C) precious
(D) supreme

TIME

Basic Words 888

動詞

Chapter 4

241~312

共
300
字

- abandon 放棄
- absorb 吸收
- accuse 指責
- achieve 達到，達成
- activate 啟動
- adapt 改編；使適合
- adopt 收養；採納
- advertise 做廣告
- affect 影響
- aim 針對；瞄準
- air 播出
- alarm 使…緊張
- amuse 娛樂，消遣
- appeal 吸引
- apply 施用
- appreciate 重視；欣賞
- approach 接近
- astonish 使…驚訝
- attach 附上
- attend 參加，出席
- attribute 歸因於
- audition 試鏡
- average 平均達到；平均計有
- ban 禁止
- bare 裸露
- believe 信仰，信奉
- benefit 對…有益，裨益
- blanket（厚厚地）覆蓋

- boast 誇耀，吹噓
- book 訂（票）
- boost 增加；推動
- bother 煩擾，使不安
- burst 突然發出（火焰，笑聲等）
- catch on 流行，風行
- celebrate 慶祝
- censor 檢查或刪剪
- channel 導引
- charge 指控，控告
- cheat 作弊
- circulate 流通，流動
- cite 引用
- claim 宣稱
- clash 不合；碰撞
- come up with 想出
- commit 犯（罪）
- compete 競爭
- complain 抱怨
- complement 補充，補足
- compliment 恭維，稱讚
- concede 承認；讓步
- concentrate 專心，集中注意
- conquer 征服
- conserve 保存；節約
- convert 改變信仰
- convey 傳達

□ convince 說服

□ counterfeit 偽造

□ crawl 爬；慢慢移動

□ crouch 蹲伏

□ crush 壓碎，壓壞

□ curse 咒罵，詛咒

■ deal 處理，對付

□ deceive 欺騙

□ declare 宣告

□ decline 下降，衰退

□ dedicate 致力，奉獻

□ defeat 擊敗

□ defend 為…辯護；防禦

□ define 下定義

□ deliver 傳遞

□ demonstrate 示範，說明

□ deprive 剝奪

B
C
D
E
F
G
H
I
J
K
L
M

□²⁴¹ **abandon** [ə`bændən] (v.) 放棄

After 72 hours they abandoned their search for the lost boy.
他們在七十二小時後放棄了對失蹤男孩的搜尋。

□²⁴² **absorb** [əb`sɔrb] (v.) 吸收

Vitamins help your body absorb what you eat.
維他命可以幫助身體吸收你吃下的東西。

◆□²⁴³ **accuse** [ə`kjuz] (v.) 指責

The woman accused her husband of being dishonest to her.
這個女人指責丈夫對她不誠實。

□²⁴⁴ **achieve** [ə`tʃiv] (v.) 達到，達成

What do you want to achieve during this semester?
你在這學期想達成什麼？

| abandon | absorb | accuse | achieve |

□²⁴⁵ **activate** [`æktə,vet] (v.) 啟動

You need to call this phone number to activate your credit card.
您必須打這個電話號碼來啟用信用卡。

□²⁴⁶ **adapt** [ə`dæpt] (v.) 改編;使適合

The director is considering adapting the story into a movie.
導演考慮將這個故事改編成電影。

□²⁴⁷ **adopt** [ə`dɑpt] (v.) 收養;採納

My parents adopted me when I was two years old.
我雙親在我兩歲時收養了我。

□²⁴⁸ **advertise** [`ædvə,taɪz] (v.) 做廣告

If you want to increase your sales, you need to advertise.
如果你想增加銷售,就得打廣告。

N
O
P
Q
R
S
T
U
V
W
X
Y
Z

B
C
D
E
F
G
H
I
J
K
L
M

□²⁴⁹ **affect** [əˋfɛkt] (v.) 影響

His opposition won't affect my decision in any way.
他的反對完全不會影響我的決定。

□²⁵⁰ **aim** [em] (v.) 針對；瞄準

The tourist aimed his camera at the tiger and then took the shot.
這個觀光客拿相機瞄準老虎然後拍了張照。

□²⁵¹ **air** [ɛr] (v.) 播出

The cartoon is aired three times a week.
這個卡通每週播出三次。

□²⁵² **alarm** [əˋlɑrm] (v.) 使⋯緊張

Our parents were alarmed by the number of people who came to the party.
我父母因參加宴會的人數而感到緊張。

| affect | aim | air | alarm |

□²⁵³ **amuse** [ə`mjuz] (v.) 娛樂，消遣

When I'm bored, I'll amuse myself by painting.
無聊的時候，我會畫畫來消遣。

□²⁵⁴ **appeal** [ə`pil] (v.) 吸引

This magazine will appeal to fashionable young people.
這本雜誌將會吸引追求流行的年輕人。

□²⁵⁵ **apply** [ə`plaɪ] (v.) 施用

If you apply pressure to a block of ice, it will melt faster.
如果在冰塊上施以壓力，它會溶得更快。

□²⁵⁶ **appreciate** [ə`priʃɪˌet] (v.) 重視；欣賞

He feels that his work is not appreciated by his boss.
他覺得老闆不重視他的工作。

amuse　　appeal　　apply　　appreciate

□²⁵⁷ **approach** [əˋprotʃ] (v.) 接近

The cowboy slowly approached the wild bull.
那個牛仔慢慢地接近野牛。

◆□²⁵⁸ **astonish** [əˋstɑnɪʃ] (v.) 使⋯驚訝

I was astonished by the number of people in the audience.
我對觀眾的人數感到驚訝。

□²⁵⁹ **attach** [əˋtætʃ] (v.) 附上

Can you attach the file to an e-mail and send it to me?
你能將檔案附在電子郵件中傳送給我嗎？

□²⁶⁰ **attend** [əˋtɛnd] (v.) 參加，出席

We attend church every Wednesday night.
我們每週三晚上參加教會活動。

◆ □²⁶¹ **attribute** [ə`trɪbjʊt] (v.) 歸因於

Actors attribute much of a movie's success to their own performances.
演員會將電影的成功歸因於自身的表現。

◆ □²⁶² **audition** [ɔ`dɪʃən] (v.) 試鏡

I'm going to audition for a part in that play.
我要去試鏡爭取那齣戲裡的一個角色。

□²⁶³ **average** [`ævərɪdʒ] (v.) 平均達到；平均計有

He averaged 31 points a game last season.
他在上一季每場球賽平均得三十一分。

□²⁶⁴ **ban** [bæn] (v.) 禁止

If a book is banned, it tends to become even more popular.
如果一本書被禁，它往往會變得更受歡迎。

N O P Q R S T U V W X Y Z

| attribute | audition | average | ban |

動詞

□²⁶⁵ **bare** [bɛr] (v.) 裸露

He bared his back to show us his big tattoo.
他裸露後背給我們看他那一大片刺青。

□²⁶⁶ **believe** [bə`liv] (v.) 信仰，信奉

Many people join a church so they can have something to believe in.
很多人加入教會，以求可以信仰的東西。

□²⁶⁷ **benefit** [`bɛnəfɪt] (v.) 對…有益，裨益

It will benefit your health greatly if you can quit smoking.
要是你能戒菸，對你的健康會很有益。

□²⁶⁸ **blanket** [`blæŋkɪt] (v.) （厚厚地）覆蓋

During the winter months, the mountains are blanketed by snow.
冬天的那幾個月，山上都被白雪覆蓋。

| bare | believe | benefit | blanket |

□ 269 **boast** [bost] (v.) 誇耀，吹噓

Jim is always boasting about how much money he makes.
吉姆總是在吹噓他賺了多少錢。

□ 270 **book** [bʊk] (v.) 訂（票）

I've already booked my flight to Hong Kong.
我已經訂了到香港的班機。

◆ □ 271 **boost** [bust] (v.) 增加；推動

The department store is offering large discounts to boost sales.
這家百貨公司以大打折來增加銷售。

□ 272 **bother** [ˈbɑðɚ] (v.) 煩擾，使不安

It really bothers me when people call and don't leave messages!
有人打電話給我卻不留言真煩人。

| boast | book | boost | bother |

A
B
C
D
E
F
G
H
I
J
K
L
M

□ [273] **burst** [bɜst] (v.) 突然發出（火焰，笑聲等）

The car burst into flames, and no one could put it out.
車子突然燒了起來，沒人能撲滅。

□ [274] **catch on** [kætʃ ɑn] (v.) 流行，風行

Those new WAP phones caught on really quickly.
這些新的無線上網手機很快就流行起來了。

□ [275] **celebrate** [ˈsɛlə,bret] (v.) 慶祝

It's my birthday! Let's celebrate!
今天是我的生日！我們來慶祝吧！

◆□ [276] **censor** [ˈsɛnsə] (v.) 檢查或刪剪

Many R-rated movies are censored for television.
許多限制級電影在電視播映前都會被刪剪。

| burst | catch on | celebrate | censor |

□²⁷⁷ **channel** [ˈtʃænl] (v.) 導引

Ted's teacher encouraged him to channel his curiosity into research.
泰德的老師鼓勵他將他的好奇心導向研究。

□²⁷⁸ **charge** [tʃɑrdʒ] (v.) 指控，控告

She's been charged with murdering her husband.
她被控謀殺親夫。

□²⁷⁹ **cheat** [tʃit] (v.) 作弊

If the teacher catches you cheating, you'll fail the test.
如果被老師抓到你考試作弊，你就會不及格。

□²⁸⁰ **circulate** [ˈsɝkjəˌlet] (v.) 流通，流動

Air circulates through the building, cooling all of the rooms.
空氣流通整棟建築，使所有的房間涼爽起來。

| channel | charge | cheat | circulate |

□²⁸¹ **cite** [saɪt] (v.) 引用

The mayor cited the latest crime figures as proof of the need for more police.
市長引用最新的犯罪數據來證明需要更多的警察。

□²⁸² **claim** [klem] (v.) 宣稱

My kid brother claims that he is the fastest runner in his class.
我小弟聲稱自己是班上跑得最快的人。

◆□²⁸³ **clash** [klæʃ] (v.) 不合;碰撞

Those colors really clash!
那些顏色真的很不協調。

□²⁸⁴ **come up with** [kʌm ʌp wɪð] (v.) 想出

Where do you come up with these crazy stories?
你這些瘋狂的故事都是怎麼想出來的?

| cite | claim | clash | come up with |

□ 285 **commit** [kə`mɪt] (v.) 犯（罪）

My mother said that if I commit too many sins I won't go to heaven.
我母親說如果我犯太多罪就不能上天堂。

□ 286 **compete** [kəm`pit] (v.) 競爭

Several advertising agencies are competing to get the contract.
好幾家廣告公司在爭那一紙合約。

□ 287 **complain** [kəm`plen] (v.) 抱怨

Bill does nothing but complain about his job.
比爾就只會抱怨他的工作。

◆ □ 288 **complement** [`kɑmplə,mɛnt] (v.) 補充，補足

They're a great couple because they complement each other.
因為互補的緣故，他們是一對神仙眷侶。

| commit | compete | complain | complement |

A
B
C
D
E
F
G
H
I
J
K
L
M

◆ □²⁸⁹ **compliment** [ˋkɑmpləˏmɛnt] (v.) 恭維，稱讚

Allow me to compliment you on your marvelous performance tonight.
我要為你今晚精彩的表演向你致意。

◆ □²⁹⁰ **concede** [kənˋsid] (v.) 承認；讓步

The computer programmer conceded that there might be bugs in his software.
電腦程式設計師承認他設計的軟體中可能有毛病。

□²⁹¹ **concentrate** [ˋkɑnsənˏtret] (v.) 專心，集中注意

I think we should concentrate on the main problem.
我覺得我們應該專注在主要的問題上。

□²⁹² **conquer** [ˋkɑŋkə] (v.) 征服

Mankind has always dreamed of conquering outer space.
人類一直夢想征服外太空。

compliment | concede | concentrate | conquer

☐²⁹³ **conserve** [kən`sɜv] (v.) 保存；節約

We should conserve natural resources for future generations.
我們應該為後代保存天然資源。

◆☐²⁹⁴ **convert** [kən`vɜt] (v.) 改變信仰

Many of my friends converted to Buddhism while in college.
我有許多朋友在大學時改信佛教。

☐²⁹⁵ **convey** [kən`ve] (v.) 傳達

I'm trying hard to think of how I should convey my new idea to my boss.
我正努力想辦法將新點子傳達給老闆。

◆☐²⁹⁶ **convince** [kən`vɪns] (v.) 說服

I tried to convince him not to drop out of school, but he wouldn't listen.
我試著說服他別休學，但他不聽。

| conserve | convert | convey | convince |

A
B
C
D
E
F
G
H
I
J
K
L
M

◆□²⁹⁷ **counterfeit** [ˈkaʊntɚfɪt] (v.) 偽造

They were convicted of counterfeiting $100 bills.
他們因偽造百元美鈔被判有罪。

◆□²⁹⁸ **crawl** [krɔl] (v.) 爬；慢慢移動

How old was your baby when he learned to crawl?
你的寶寶多大開始學爬？

◆□²⁹⁹ **crouch** [kraʊtʃ] (v.) 蹲伏

Some animals crouch in tall grass to wait for the chance to jump on their prey.
有些動物蹲伏在長草中等待撲食獵物的機會。

◆□³⁰⁰ **crush** [krʌʃ] (v.) 壓碎，壓壞

Pick up the bug gently. You don't want to crush it.
輕輕地拿起這隻蟲。不要壓碎牠。

| counterfeit | crawl | crouch | crush |

◆ □³⁰¹ **curse** [kɜs] (v.) 咒罵，詛咒

John cursed after he cut his hand.
約翰割傷手之後出口咒罵。

□³⁰² **deal** [dil] (v.) 處理，對付

It will take us a few hours to deal with this problem.
我們將得花幾個小時來處理這個問題。

◆ □³⁰³ **deceive** [dɪˋsiv] (v.) 欺騙

She was deceived by the man in uniform—she really thought he was a police officer.
她被那個穿制服的人騙了──她真以為他是個警察。

□³⁰⁴ **declare** [dɪˋklɛr] (v.) 宣告

The 13 colonies declared independence in 1776.
這十三個殖民地在一七七六年宣告獨立。

| curse | deal | deceive | declare |

動詞

□ 305 **decline** [dɪˋklaɪn] (v.) 下降，衰退

After 35, one's health begins to decline
三十五歲以後，人的健康就開始走下坡。

□ 306 **dedicate** [ˋdɛdə‚ket] (v.) 致力，奉獻

He has dedicated his life to scientific
research.
他一生致力於科學研究。

□ 307 **defeat** [dɪˋfit] (v.) 擊敗

NATO forces defeated all local resistance.
北大西洋公約組織的軍隊擊敗了當地所有的反抗勢
力。

□ 308 **defend** [dɪˋfɛnd] (v.) 為⋯辯護；防禦

I'll defend Tom because he's my brother.
我會為湯姆辯護，因為他是我兄弟。

□³⁰⁹ **define** [dɪˋfaɪn] (v.) 下定義

It's hard to define what my ideal job would be.
要我為理想的工作下定義是件困難的事。

□³¹⁰ **deliver** [dɪˋlɪvə] (v.) 傳遞

I'll deliver the message to Mr. Lee myself.
我會親自將這個訊息傳達給李先生。

□³¹¹ **demonstrate** [ˋdɛmən͵stret] (v.) 示範，說明

I can demonstrate this physical law with a simple experiment.
我可以用一個簡單的實驗來示範這項物理定律。

◆□³¹² **deprive** [dɪˋpraɪv] (v.) 剝奪

Don't deprive yourself of fun while you're in college.
讀大學時不要剝奪自己玩樂的機會。

N
O
P
Q
R
S
T
U
V
W
X
Y
Z

「字」我挑戰 4

解答請見 p. 290

_____ 1. Even though the weather was terrible, the letter carrier had to _____ the mail.
(A) adopt
(B) channel
(C) boast
(D) deliver

_____ 2. Please _____ my message to your colleagues.
(A) convey
(B) decline
(C) activate
(D) audition

_____ 3. The loud music _____ the student, who was trying to read.
(A) clashed
(B) defended
(C) bothered
(D) achieved

_____ 4. It's unclear whether this new style of notebook computers will _____.
(A) deal with
(B) catch on
(C) believe in
(D) come up with

_____ 5. Don't _____ about your problem; do something about it!
(A) complain
(B) absorb
(C) alarm
(D) defeat

_____ 6. The archer _____ carefully before he released the arrow.
(A) crawled
(B) devoted
(C) attended
(D) aimed

_____ 7. I agree with you, but are you sure you can _____ the boss that you're right?
(A) define
(B) accuse
(C) convince
(D) boost

_____ 8. Since we're out of money, we'll have to _____ our original plan.
(A) curse
(B) abandon
(C) deprive
(D) amuse

_____ 9. Be careful not to _____ the bananas
when you put down those books.
(A) conserve
(B) adapt
(C) crush
(D) astonish

_____10. I never _____ I was an expert at using
computers.
(A) claimed
(B) defined
(C) applied
(D) chatted

_____11. Everyone _____ Bill on his excellent
presentation.
(A) complemented
(B) demonstrated
(C) appreciated
(D) complimented

_____12. The general said he would never _____
defeat.
(A) convert
(B) burst
(C) concede
(D) censor

TIME
Basic Words 888

動詞

Chapter 5

313~384

共
300
字

□ devise　想出；設計

□ devote　奉獻，投入

□ diagnose　診斷

□ die out　滅絕

□ disguise　偽裝

□ dispel　排除，驅散

□ dispute　爭論，辯論

□ disrupt　擾亂

□ distinguish　使出眾，使與眾不同

□ distribute　發行；分配

□ dominate　主導，支配

□ download　下載

□ drift　漂

□ drop out　輟學

□ duplicate　複製

■ embrace　擁抱

□ emerge　出現；浮出

□ energize　供給能量

□ enforce　強制執行

□ enrich　使豐富

□ enroll　登記，註冊

□ ensure　確保

□ entertain　使快樂；款待

□ entitle　使有權利；以…為名

□ entrust　委託

□ equip　配備

□ estimate　估計

□ evolve　發展；演進

□ excel　過人，勝過

□ exist　存在

□ expand　擴展

□ expire　到期，屆滿

□ explode　爆炸

□ explore　探測

□ expose　使接觸；暴露

□ express　表達

□ extend　延長，延伸

■ faint　昏厥

□ fasten　固定

□ feature　以…為號召

□ fertilize　施肥

□ figure　料想；推斷

□ float　飄浮；漂流

□ flock　群聚

□ flood　淹沒，淹水

□ flunk　當掉

□ focus　專注

□ fool around　打混，無所事事

□ frown　皺眉

□ fulfill　達成，履行

□ fuse　融合

■ gain　獲得

□ generate　生產

□ greet　迎接

□ grind　研磨

- ■ handle 處理
- □ harvest 收穫
- □ head 領導
- □ heal 治癒
- □ hesitate 猶豫
- □ highlight 凸顯
- □ hire 雇用
- □ hook 使…上癮；勾住
- □ host 主持
- □ hug 擁抱
- ■ identify 與…認同；辨認
- □ ignore 忽視
- □ illustrate 說明
- □ imitate 模仿
- □ imply 暗示
- □ import 進口
- □ indicate 表示

動詞

□ 313 **devise** [dɪˋvaɪz] (v.) 想出；設計

The robbers spent days devising a plan to rob the bank.

搶匪們花了幾天時間策畫搶銀行。

□ 314 **devote** [dɪˋvot] (v.) 奉獻，投入

Our research team devoted two months to this project.

我們的研究團隊投入兩個月的時間在這項計畫上。

□ 315 **diagnose** [ˌdaɪəgˋnoz] (v.) 診斷

No one has been able to diagnose my illness.

一直沒人能診斷出我的病。

□ 316 **die out** [daɪ aʊt] (v.) 滅絕

Dinosaurs died out millions of years ago.

恐龍在數百萬年前就滅絕了。

| devise | devote | diagnose | die out |

□³¹⁷ **disguise** [dɪsˋgaɪz] (v.) 偽裝

The bank robber was disguised as a security guard.
銀行搶匪偽裝成警衛。

◆□³¹⁸ **dispel** [dɪˋspɛl] (v.) 排除，驅散

The sun dispelled the fog.
太陽驅散了霧氣。

□³¹⁹ **dispute** [dɪˋspjut] (v.) 爭論，辯論

The two countries have disputed that stretch of land for years.
這兩國已經為那片土地爭論很多年了。

◆□³²⁰ **disrupt** [dɪsˋrʌpt] (v.) 擾亂

Protesters disrupted the press conference.
抗議者擾亂了記者會。

N
O
P
Q
R
S
T
U
V
W
X
Y
Z

| disguise | dispel | dispute | disrupt |

A
B
C

D
E

F
G
H
I
J
K
L
M

□³²¹ **distinguish** [dɪˋstɪŋgwɪʃ] (v.) 使出眾，使與眾不同

Our company has distinguished itself in the field of science.
我們公司在科學界表現傑出。

◆□³²² **distribute** [dɪˋstrɪbjut] (v.) 發行；分配

This magazine is distributed in Taiwan, Hong Kong and Singapore.
這份雜誌在台灣、香港和新加坡發行。

□³²³ **dominate** [ˋdɑməˏnet] (v.) 主導，支配

Sara always dominates the conversation.
莎拉總是談話的主導者。

□³²⁴ **download** [ˋdaʊnˏlod] (v.) 下載

Listen to this music I just downloaded from the Internet!
聽聽看我剛從網路上下載的音樂！

□³²⁵ **drift** [drɪft] (v.) 漂

If we turn off the boat's motor, we can drift towards the shore.
如果將船的發動機關掉，我們就會朝岸邊漂去。

□³²⁶ **drop out** [drɑp aʊt] (v.) 輟學

He dropped out of college to join a rock and roll band.
他大學時輟學，加入了搖滾樂團。

□³²⁷ **duplicate** [ˈdjuplə͵ket] (v.) 複製

I want you to go to this meeting and duplicate the wonderful speech you gave last week. 我要你參加這場會議，將上週所作的完美演講重講一次。

□³²⁸ **embrace** [ɪmˈbres] (v.) 擁抱

They were oblivious to the outside world as they embraced each other on the station platform.
他們在車站月台上擁抱時對周遭渾然不覺。

| drift | drop out | duplicate | embrace |

動詞

□ 329 **emerge** [ɪˋmɝdʒ] (v.) 出現;浮出

It will be interesting to see who emerges as the next leader of Taiwan.
看看誰會脫穎而出成為台灣下一任的領導人會很有趣。

□ 330 **energize** [ˋɛnɚ͵dʒaɪz] (v.) 供給能量

Try some of this drink—it will energize you!
試試這個飲料——它會給你帶來活力!

□ 331 **enforce** [ɪnˋfɔrs] (v.) 強制執行

It's difficult to enforce the new no-smoking policy.
要強制執行新的禁菸政策很困難。

□ 332 **enrich** [ɪnˋrɪtʃ] (v.) 使豐富

Reading has enriched my life.
讀書豐富我的生命。

emerge　energize　enforce　enrich

□³³³ **enroll** [ɪn`rol] (v.) 登記，註冊

I want to enroll in an art class so I can learn to draw.
我要登記參加藝術課程學畫畫。

□³³⁴ **ensure** [ɪn`ʃʊr] (v.) 確保

Mail your package early to ensure that it arrives before Christmas.
早點寄出你的包裹以確保它能在聖誕節前送達。

□³³⁵ **entertain** [ˌɛntə`ten] (v.) 使快樂；款待

He really likes to entertain other people—he should be an actor.
他真是喜歡娛樂別人——他應該當演員的。

□³³⁶ **entitle** [ɪn`taɪtl] (v.) 使有權利；以…為名

This ticket entitles you to a free seat at the concert.
這張票可以使你有一個演唱會的免費座位。

| enroll | ensure | entertain | entitle |

A
B
C
D
E
F
G
H
I
J
K
L
M

◆ □³³⁷ **entrust** [ɪnˋtrʌst] (v.) 委託

He didn't look like the kind of man you should entrust your luggage to.
他看起來不像是那種你可以委託行李的人。

□³³⁸ **equip** [ɪˋkwɪp] (v.) 配備

This car is equipped with a Hi-Fi stereo CD player.
這款車配備有高傳真立體 CD 唱機。

□³³⁹ **estimate** [ˋɛstə‚met] (v.) 估計

We estimate that the company will be worth two million after a year.
我們估計這家公司在一年後將有兩百萬的價值。

□³⁴⁰ **evolve** [ɪˋvɑlv] (v.) 發展；演進

The software industry has evolved into a multi-billion dollar industry.
軟體業已經發展為好幾十億美元的產業。

| entrust | equip | estimate | evolve |

◆ ☐[341] **excel** [ɪkˋsɛl] (v.) 過人，勝過

Children of scientists often excel in the areas of math and science.
科學家的小孩常常在數理方面表現傑出。

☐[342] **exist** [ɪgˋzɪst] (v.) 存在

Many people believe that ghosts really exist.
許多人相信鬼魂確實存在。

☐[343] **expand** [ɪkˋspænd] (v.) 擴展

Our company is going to expand into the European market.
我們公司即將擴展到歐洲市場。

☐[344] **expire** [ɪkˋspaɪr] (v.) 到期，屆滿

My visa expires on the 3rd of next month.
我的簽證在下個月三號到期。

| excel | exist | expand | expire |

A
B
C
D
E
F
G
H
I
J
K
L
M

◆□³⁴⁵ **explode** [ɪk`splod] (v.) 爆炸

The car crashed into the wall and then exploded.

那輛車子撞上圍牆然後爆炸。

◆□³⁴⁶ **explore** [ɪk`splor] (v.) 探測

We spent the whole day exploring the countryside.

我們花了一整天的時間在鄉間探勘。

◆□³⁴⁷ **expose** [ɪk`spoz] (v.) 使接觸；暴露

Since I grew up in Paris, I was exposed to the French language at a very young age.

因為我是在巴黎長大的，我很小就身處在法語的環境中。

□³⁴⁸ **express** [ɪk`sprɛs] (v.) 表達

Some people are not very good at expressing themselves.

有些人不善於表達自己。

| explode | explore | expose | express |

□ 349 **extend** [ɪk`stɛnd] (v.) 延長，延伸

I need to go to the police office to extend my visa.
我得到警察局去延長我的簽證。

□ 350 **faint** [fent] (v.) 昏厥

When I saw his bloody hand, I fainted.
當我看到他血淋淋的手時，我昏了過去。

□ 351 **fasten** [`fæsn̩] (v.) 固定

You need to fasten your seatbelt before we get on the highway.
在我們上公路之前，你得繫好安全帶。

□ 352 **feature** [`fitʃɚ] (v.) 以…為號召

The new movie features Tom Cruise and Nicole Kidman.
這部新電影以湯姆克魯斯和妮可基嫚為號召。

| extend | faint | fasten | feature |

◆□³⁵³ **fertilize** [ˋfɝtḷ͵aɪz] (v.) 施肥

If this soil isn't fertilized, a garden will never grow.
這片土壤如果不施肥，花園將永遠長不出來。

□³⁵⁴ **figure** [ˋfɪgjɚ] (v.) 料想；推斷

I figured you'd be hungry, so I bought you this snack.
我想你可能會餓，所以我替你買了這份點心。

□³⁵⁵ **float** [flot] (v.) 飄浮；漂流

Oil doesn't mix with water; it simply floats on top.
油不會與水混合；它只會浮在水面上。

□³⁵⁶ **flock** [flɑk] (v.) 群聚

Hundreds of photographers flocked around 1976 after the concert.
演唱會後數以百計的攝影師群聚在 1976 合唱團身邊。

| fertilize | figure | float | flock |

□ [357] **flood** [flʌd] (v.) 淹沒，淹水

Fans flooded the concert hall, all waiting to ask Faye Wang for an autograph.
歌迷淹沒音樂廳，等著索取王菲的簽名。

□ [358] **flunk** [flʌŋk] (v.) 當掉

There are many rich people who flunked out of school.
許多有錢人都曾被學校退學。

□ [359] **focus** [ˋfokəs] (v.) 專注

When I'm tired, I can't focus on my work.
我感到疲倦時就無法專注在工作上。

□ [360] **fool around** [ful əˋraʊnd] (v.) 打混，無所事事

All I did today was fool around at the mall.
我今天所做的事就是在購物中心閒晃而已。

| flood | flunk | focus | fool around |

動詞

◆ □³⁶¹ **frown** [fraʊn] (v.) 皺眉

She's frowning because she doesn't know the answer.

她皺著眉，因為不知道答案。

□³⁶² **fulfill** [fʊlˋfɪl] (v.) 達成，履行

His dream was fulfilled when he finally got to New York.

他終於來到紐約，達成了夢想。

◆ □³⁶³ **fuse** [fjuz] (v.) 融合

My goal is to fuse the best parts of Chinese and Western music together.

我的目標是將中西音樂的精華融合在一起。

□³⁶⁴ **gain** [ɡen] (v.) 獲得

The prisoner gained freedom after serving out his time.

囚犯刑期服滿後獲得了自由。

| frown | fulfill | fuse | gain |

□³⁶⁵ **generate** [ˈdʒɛnəˌret] (v.) 生產

This machine can generate electricity from the sun.
這部機器可以利用太陽能發電。

□³⁶⁶ **greet** [grit] (v.) 迎接

A beautiful girl in a Kimono greeted us at the front gate of the temple.
一位身著和服的美麗女孩在廟門口迎接我們。

◆□³⁶⁷ **grind** [graɪnd] (v.) 研磨

The Chinese doctor ground the medicine into a fine powder.
中醫師把藥磨成細粉。

□³⁶⁸ **handle** [ˈhændl] (v.) 處理

If you can't handle your job, it's time to quit.
如果你無法處理你的工作，該是你辭職的時候了。

| generate | greet | grind | handle |

動詞

◆ □369 **harvest** [`harvɪst] (v.) 收穫
We harvest the corn every September.
我們每年九月收割穀物。

□370 **head** [hɛd] (v.) 領導
We need someone to head the company's new department.
我們需要有人來領導公司的新部門。

◆ □371 **heal** [hil] (v.) 治癒
The body has an amazing ability to heal itself.
身體有神奇的自療能力。

□372 **hesitate** [`hɛzə,tet] (v.) 猶豫
I hesitated a while before accepting his marriage proposal.
接受他求婚前，我猶豫了一下。

A B C D E F G H I J K L M

| harvest | head | heal | hesitate |

□³⁷³ **highlight** [`haɪ,laɪt] (v.) 凸顯

The ad highlights the reliability of this new car.
這則廣告凸顯出這款新車的可靠性。

□³⁷⁴ **hire** [haɪr] (v.) 雇用

The tourists hired a guide for the day.
這些觀光客雇用了一名導遊一天的時間。

□³⁷⁵ **hook** [hʊk] (v.) 使…上癮；勾住

Play Quake III once, and you'll be hooked for life.
玩一次「雷神之鎚」，你就會終身上癮。

□³⁷⁶ **host** [host] (v.) 主持

She used to host a famous TV show.
她從前主持過一個出名的電視節目。

N O P Q R S T U V W X Y Z

| highlight | hire | hook | host |

A
B
C
D
E
F
G
H
I
J
K
L
M

□ 377 **hug** [hʌg] (v.) 擁抱

Medical research has proven that being hugged every day improves your health.
醫學報告證明每天被人擁抱有益健康。

□ 378 **identify** [aɪˋdɛntəˌfaɪ] (v.) 與⋯認同；辨認

I can identify with her because I had the same experience.
因為有過相同的經驗，所以我能夠認同她。

□ 379 **ignore** [ɪgˋnɔr] (v.) 忽視

You can't ignore the fact that he likes you.
妳不能忽視他喜歡妳的事實。

□ 380 **illustrate** [ˋɪləstret] (v.) 說明

The professor uses a lot of examples to illustrate his point.
教授舉了很多例子來說明他的論點。

| hug | identify | ignore | illustrate |

□³⁸¹ **imitate** [ˋɪmə,tet] (v.) 模仿

She likes to go to KTV and imitate famous singers.

她喜歡到 KTV 模仿名歌星唱歌。

□³⁸² **imply** [ɪmˋplaɪ] (v.) 暗示

Are you implying that I am not a good boss?

你在暗示我不是一個好老闆嗎？

□³⁸³ **import** [ɪmˋport] (v.) 進口

We imported almost all of our furniture from Thailand.

我們全部的家具幾乎都從泰國進口。

□³⁸⁴ **indicate** [ˋɪndə,ket] (v.) 表示

When this light comes on, it indicates you need to add oil.

這個燈亮起時表示你需要添加油料了。

N O P Q R S T U V W X Y Z

「字」我挑戰 5

解答請見 p. 290

_____ 1. It was so hot outside, I almost _____.
  (A) emerged
  (B) infected
  (C) fainted
  (D) healed

_____ 2. Michael Jordan _____ basketball during the 1990s.
  (A) dominated
  (B) enforced
  (C) imitated
  (D) exploded

_____ 3. The teacher told the students not to _____ in the hallways.
  (A) drop out
  (B) flunk
  (C) fool around
  (D) evolve

_____ 4. As the company grew, it _____ more employees.
  (A) dispelled
  (B) imported
  (C) downloaded
  (D) hired

_____ 5. At the restaurant, employees _____ customers when they come in.
(A) highlight
(B) disrupt
(C) extend
(D) greet

_____ 6. Thousands of people _____ to the department store during the post-holiday sales.
(A) distributed
(B) flocked
(C) explored
(D) fused

_____ 7. Its sail destroyed by the storm, the small boat _____ helplessly in the ocean.
(A) exposed
(B) entitled
(C) drifted
(D) fastened

_____ 8. If you need my help, please don't _____ to ask.
(A) hesitate
(B) disguise
(C) ensure
(D) express

_____ 9. As this chart _____, our sales are down 23% this year.
   (A) distinguishes
   (B) indicates
   (C) exists
   (D) fulfills

_____10. The farmers worked hard to _____ the fields before the rain came again.
   (A) diagnose
   (B) estimate
   (C) ignore
   (D) harvest

_____11. Because Emily can't _____ on any one task, she never gets anything done.
   (A) focus
   (B) identify
   (C) duplicate
   (D) feature

_____12. This pass _____ you to a free movie ticket, small coke, and small popcorn.
   (A) energizes
   (B) enrolls
   (C) entitles
   (D) gains

TIME
Basic Words 888

動詞

Chapter 6

385~456

共
300
字

- infect 感染
- inherit 繼承
- inhibit 抑制
- inject 注射
- inspire 激勵，啟發
- install 安裝
- instruct 指導
- insult 侮辱
- integrate 整合
- intend 打算，意圖
- invent 發明
- irritate 激怒
- issue 發出
- ■ label 加標籤，標示
- launch 推出；發射
- leak 漏
- lose one's head 失去理智；衝動
- lure 引誘
- ■ maintain 維持
- manage 設法做到
- manipulate 操縱；巧妙處理
- manufacture 生產，製造
- market 行銷
- match 和…一樣；匹配
- mention 提及，說到
- mimic 模仿
- modify 修改

- moisten 使濕潤
- mold 塑造
- ■ nibble 細咬
- nod 點頭
- nominate 提名
- ■ obtain 獲得
- occur 發生
- offend 得罪，冒犯
- operate 操作
- organize 籌辦；安排
- overdo 做得太過火
- overlook 忽略
- ■ participate 參與
- patent 申請專利
- pay off 成功，得到應得的代價
- persevere 堅持
- persuade 說服
- pinpoint 準確指出
- polish 擦亮
- pollute 污染
- portray 飾演；描繪
- post 張貼
- predict 預言，預測
- preserve 保存
- promote 促銷，宣傳
- protest 抗議
- publish 出版，發行
- purchase 購買

- □ purify 淨化
- ■ quote 引用
- ■ raise 養育，栽培
- □ recall 想起，回想
- □ recognize 認出
- □ recover 復原，恢復
- □ reduce 減少，降低
- □ reflect 反映
- □ regulate 管制，整頓
- □ rehearse 排練
- □ reject 拒絕
- □ release 發表；釋放
- □ remain 剩下；留下
- □ remodel 改建，重新塑造
- □ remove 去除；脫下
- □ replace 替換；取代
- □ reply 回覆

□385 **infect** [ɪnˋfɛkt] (v.) 感染

If you don't keep the wound clean, it might get infected.
傷口如果不保持清潔可能會感染。

□386 **inherit** [ɪnˋhɛrɪt] (v.) 繼承

I inherited a small piece of land from my uncle.
我從叔父那裡繼承了一小片土地。

◆ □387 **inhibit** [ɪnˋhɪbɪt] (v.) 抑制

The drug will inhibit the progress of the disease.
藥物會抑制病情的發展。

□388 **inject** [ɪnˋdʒɛkt] (v.) 注射

Injected medicines usually take effect faster than swallowed ones.
注射藥通常比口服藥快生效。

| infect | inherit | inhibit | inject |

□ 389 **inspire** [ɪnˋspaɪr] (v.) 激勵，啓發

I am inspired by everything that you have been able to accomplish.
每件你做到的事情都激勵了我。

□ 390 **install** [ɪnˋstɔl] (v.) 安裝

Can you help me install this software?
你能幫我安裝這個軟體嗎？

□ 391 **instruct** [ɪnˋstrʌkt] (v.) 指導

That fitness coach has instructed quite a few movie stars.
那位健身教練指導過好幾位電影明星。

□ 392 **insult** [ɪnˋsʌlt] (v.) 侮辱

I was doing you a favor. Please don't insult me by offering me money.
我是在幫你的忙。請別付錢來侮辱我。

N
O
P
Q
R
S
T
U
V
W
X
Y
Z

| inspire | install | instruct | insult |

動詞

□³⁹³ **integrate** [ˋɪntəˏgret] (v.) 整合

The Japanese architect integrates both Western and Eastern styles.
這位日本建築師結合了東西方的風格。

□³⁹⁴ **intend** [ɪnˋtɛnd] (v.) 打算，意圖

When I first came to Tainan, I didn't intend to stay here for long.
我剛來到台南時，並沒有打算要留在這裡很久。

□³⁹⁵ **invent** [ɪnˋvɛnt] (v.) 發明

I wish someone would invent a way to make the day longer than 24 hours!
我希望有人能發明一個方法，讓一天不只二十四個小時！

□³⁹⁶ **irritate** [ˋɪrəˏtet] (v.) 激怒

If you want to irritate him, just call him Shorty.
想要激怒他，只要叫他「矮子」就行了。

| integrate | intend | invent | irritate |

□³⁹⁷ **issue** [ˈɪʃju] (v.) 發出

The police issue heavy fines to drunk drivers.
警察對酒醉駕車的人開出很重的罰金。

□³⁹⁸ **label** [ˈlebl] (v.) 加標籤，標示

Companies are required to label what's in food items.
公司被要求將食品項目的成分標示出來。

□³⁹⁹ **launch** [lɔntʃ] (v.) 推出；發射

We launched a new makeup line last month.
我們上個月推出一系列新的化妝產品。

□⁴⁰⁰ **leak** [lik] (v.) 漏

The car leaked oil all over the drive.
那輛車漏得整條路都是油。

B
C
D
E
F
G
H
I
J
K

□⁴⁰¹ **lose one's head** (v.) 失去理智；衝動

Even though they were under threat of death, they didn't lose their heads.
他們雖然飽受死亡威脅，卻沒有失去理智。

◆□⁴⁰² **lure** [lʊr] (v.) 引誘

You can lure the dog to you with a bone.
你可以用骨頭引誘那隻狗過來。

□⁴⁰³ **maintain** [men`ten] (v.) 維持

It's difficult to maintain your English ability if you don't practice every day.
如果你不每天練習，就難以維持英文能力。

□⁴⁰⁴ **manage** [`mænɪdʒ] (v.) 設法做到

After 6 hours, we finally managed to get my brother's room clean.
經過了六小時後，我們終於把我哥哥的房間整理乾淨了。

◆ □⁴⁰⁵ **manipulate** [mə`nɪpjə,let] (v.) 操縱；巧妙處理

He accused the government of manipulating public opinion.
他指控政府操縱輿論。

□⁴⁰⁶ **manufacture** [,mænjə`fæktʃə] (v.) 生產，製造

Our company manufactures car parts.
我們公司製造汽車零件。

□⁴⁰⁷ **market** [`mɑrkɪt] (v.) 行銷

We have a good product, but we need to figure out how to market it.
我們有好產品，但必須研究行銷之道。

□⁴⁰⁸ **match** [mætʃ] (v.) 和…一樣；匹配

If you give 100 dollars to charity, I'll match you.
你要是捐一百元給慈善機構，我就跟你一樣。

manipulate | manufacture | market | match

B
C
D
E
F
G
H
I
J
K
L

M

□⁴⁰⁹ **mention** [ˈmɛnʃən] (v.) 提及，說到

I forgot to mention that I am going on vacation for two weeks.
我忘記說我要去度假兩週。

◆□⁴¹⁰ **mimic** [ˈmɪmɪk] (v.) 模仿

Some birds can mimic human speech.
有些鳥類會模仿人類的語言。

□⁴¹¹ **modify** [ˈmɑdə,faɪ] (v.) 修改

We need to modify this paper a little before it can be published.
我們必須在這篇論文出版之前稍作修改。

◆□⁴¹² **moisten** [ˈmɔɪsn̩] (v.) 使濕潤

You need to moisten the stamp before you put it on the envelope.
將郵票貼在信封上之前得將它沾濕。

| mention | mimic | modify | moisten |

◆ □⁴¹³ **mold** [mold] (v.) 塑造

Plastics can be molded into any shape you like.
塑膠可以塑造成任何你要的形狀。

◆ □⁴¹⁴ **nibble** [ˋnɪbḷ] (v.) 細咬

You've been nibbling on my sandwich, haven't you?
你咬過我的三明治，是不是？

□⁴¹⁵ **nod** [nɑd] (v.) 點頭

He didn't say anything, but he nodded his head in agreement.
他不發一語，不過卻點頭表示同意。

□⁴¹⁶ **nominate** [ˋnɑmə,net] (v.) 提名

I hope to be nominated for President of the Student Council.
我希望被提名為學生會主席。

| mold | nibble | nod | nominate |

動詞

□⁴¹⁷ **obtain** [əb`ten] (v.) 獲得

You can obtain a lot of information over the Internet.
在網路上你可以獲得許多資料。

□⁴¹⁸ **occur** [ə`kɜ] (v.) 發生

I never thought an earthquake would occur while I was on vacation.
我沒想到在度假時會發生地震。

□⁴¹⁹ **offend** [ə`fɛnd] (v.) 得罪，冒犯

Just tell me your honest opinion. You won't offend me.
儘管告訴我你真正的意見。不會得罪我的。

□⁴²⁰ **operate** [`ɑpə,ret] (v.) 操作

I don't know how to operate this machine.
我不知道如何操作這部機器。

| obtain | occur | offend | operate |

□⁴²¹ **organize** [ˈɔrgənˌaɪz] (v.) 籌辦；安排

The class organized a surprise birthday party for Jane.
班上為珍妮籌辦了一個驚喜的生日宴會。

□⁴²² **overdo** [ˈovəˈdu] (v.) 做得太過火

The joke was overdone.
這個玩笑開得太過火了。

□⁴²³ **overlook** [ˌovəˈlʊk] (v.) 忽略

The boss overlooked me again this year for a raise.
老闆今年又忽略了我，沒有加薪。

□⁴²⁴ **participate** [pɑrˈtɪsəˌpet] (v.) 參與

If you participate more in class, you'll get a better grade.
如果你在課堂上參與更多，你的成績會更好。

| organize | overdo | overlook | participate |

□ [425] **patent** [ˋpætn̩t] (v.) 申請專利

You should patent your new invention before someone else thinks of the same thing.
你應該在別人想到相同的點子前，申請這項新發明的專利。

□ [426] **pay off** [pe ɔf] (v.) 成功，得到應得的代價

The stocks you told me to invest in last year really paid off.
你去年要我投資的股票真的有賺錢。

□ [427] **persevere** [͵pɝsəˋvɪr] (v.) 堅持

You must persevere, in spite of all the difficulties.
雖然困難重重，你一定要堅持到底。

□ [428] **persuade** [pɚˋswed] (v.) 說服

The students persuaded the teacher to postpone the exam.
學生們說服老師將考試延期。

□⁴²⁹ **pinpoint** [ˋpɪn,pɔɪnt] (v.) 準確指出

Firefighters always try to pinpoint the reason a fire started.
消防人員總是試著精確指出起火的原因。

□⁴³⁰ **polish** [ˋpɑlɪʃ] (v.) 擦亮

He always has his shoes polished at the railway station.
他總是在火車站讓人擦鞋。

□⁴³¹ **pollute** [pəˋlut] (v.) 污染

The best thing about bicycles is that they don't pollute the air.
腳踏車最大的好處是不會污染空氣。

□⁴³² **portray** [porˋtre] (v.) 飾演；描繪

A good actor can portray many different kinds of characters.
一位好演員能飾演許多不同類型的角色。

| pinpoint | polish | pollute | portray |

動詞

□[433] **post** [post] (v.) 張貼

The teacher posted a notice on the wall.
老師在牆上張貼了一張公告。

□[434] **predict** [prɪ`dɪkt] (v.) 預言，預測

It's hard to predict what the world will be like in twenty years.
很難預測二十年後的世界會是什麼樣子。

□[435] **preserve** [prɪ`zɜv] (v.) 保存

Italy is trying hard to preserve the Leaning Tower of Pisa.
義大利致力於保存比薩斜塔。

□[436] **promote** [prə`mot] (v.) 促銷，宣傳

The company spent millions of dollars to promote its new soda.
這家公司花了幾百萬來促銷它新上市的汽水。

| post | predict | preserve | promote |

□⁴³⁷ **protest** [prə`tɛst] (v.) 抗議

I'm going to city hall to protest the increase in taxes.
我要到市政府去抗議增稅。

□⁴³⁸ **publish** [`pʌblɪʃ] (v.) 出版，發行

I am going to publish my first book this summer.
今年夏天我將出版我的第一本書。

□⁴³⁹ **purchase** [`pɜtʃəs] (v.) 購買

After they got married, they purchased everything together.
他們在婚後總是一起購物。

□⁴⁴⁰ **purify** [`pjʊrə,faɪ] (v.) 淨化

Scientists are working hard to discover better ways of purifying ocean water.
科學家正努力尋找淨化海水的更佳方式。

| protest | publish | purchase | purify |

A
B
C
D
E
F
G
H
I
J
K
L
M

□⁴⁴¹ **quote** [kwot] (v.) 引用

To quote my mother, "All things happen for a reason."
引用我媽媽的話：「所有事情會發生都有個理由。」

□⁴⁴² **raise** [rez] (v.) 養育，栽培

She raised four children all by herself.
她獨力撫養四個子女。

□⁴⁴³ **recall** [rɪˋkɔl] (v.) 想起，回想

I don't recall ever meeting him before.
我不記得我看過他。

□⁴⁴⁴ **recognize** [ˋrɛkəɡˌnaɪz] (v.) 認出

Wow! You've really changed! I almost didn't recognize you!
哇！你真的變了！我幾乎認不出你來了！

| quote | raise | recall | recognize |

□ 445 **recover** [rɪ`kʌvɚ] (v.) 復原，恢復

It took me two weeks to recover from that terrible cold.
這場可怕的感冒花了我兩個星期時間才復原。

□ 446 **reduce** [rɪ`djus] (v.) 減少，降低

If you want to lose weight, reduce your calorie intake.
如果你要減肥，必須減少卡路里的攝取。

□ 447 **reflect** [rɪ`flɛkt] (v.) 反映

My grades don't reflect how much I learned in school.
我的成績不能反映出我在學校學到了多少。

□ 448 **regulate** [`rɛgjə,let] (v.) 管制，整頓

The Fair Trade Committee regulates trade in Taiwan.
公平交易委員會管制台灣的買賣交易。

N
O
P
Q
R
S
T
U
V
W
X
Y
Z

| recover | reduce | reflect | regulate |

A
B
C
D
E
F
G
H
I
J
K
L
M

□ [449] **rehearse** [rɪˋhɝs] (v.) 排練

She rehearsed what she would say on the telephone over and over again before she called.

在打電話前她排練了好多次要說的話。

□ [450] **reject** [rɪˋdʒɛkt] (v.) 拒絕

My boss rejected my request for a raise.

老闆拒絕了我加薪的要求。

□ [451] **release** [rɪˋlis] (v.) 發表；釋放

The new report on cancer research was released last week.

這篇癌症研究的新報告於上週發表。

□ [452] **remain** [rɪˋmen] (v.) 剩下；留下

When time was up, only three test-takers remained in the classroom.

時間到的時候，教室裡只剩下三名考生。

| rehearse | reject | release | remain |

□⁴⁵³ **remodel** [rɪˋmɑdl] (v.) 改建，重新塑造

We spent several months remodeling our house last year.
去年我們花了幾個月的時間改建我們的房子。

□⁴⁵⁴ **remove** [rɪˋmuv] (v.) 去除；脫下

This soap will remove the coffee stain on your dress.
這種肥皂可以除去妳洋裝上的咖啡污漬。

□⁴⁵⁵ **replace** [rɪˋples] (v.) 替換；取代

The clock isn't broken; the batteries just need to be replaced.
這個鐘沒有壞，只是需要換電池了。

□⁴⁵⁶ **reply** [rɪˋplaɪ] (v.) 回覆

If you don't reply to his offer, you'll miss a great chance.
如果你不回覆他的提議將會錯失良機。

N O P Q **R** S T U V W X Y Z

| remodel | remove | replace | reply |

「字」我挑戰 6

解答請見 p. 290

_____ 1. The band usually _____ three days a
week.
(A) mimics
(B) occurs
(C) publishes
(D) rehearses

_____ 2. Everyone was _____ by the president's
speech.
(A) inspired
(B) nominated
(C) issued
(D) removed

_____ 3. More companies than ever will _____ in
this year's computer show.
(A) reply
(B) manage
(C) participate
(D) manufacture

_____ 4. Do you _____ exactly when she left the
office?
(A) maintain
(B) nod
(C) recall
(D) predict

_____ 5. The streets would be safer if we could
_____ the number of motorcycles being
driven.
(A) request
(B) reduce
(C) launch
(D) match

_____ 6. I _____ a hundred thousand dollars from
a cousin I don't even know!
(A) inherited
(B) manipulated
(C) purchased
(D) regulated

_____ 7. The mouse _____ on a piece of cheese.
(A) rejected
(B) polished
(C) integrated
(D) nibbled

_____ 8. When we moved, we _____ each box
according to what room it belonged in.
(A) modified
(B) labeled
(C) overdid
(D) quoted

_____ 9. I was the only one who _____ in the theater to watch the ending credits.
(A) intended
(B) persevered
(C) lured
(D) remained

_____10. Please _____ this towel and use it to wipe off the table.
(A) operate
(B) raise
(C) moisten
(D) inject

_____11.Whatever you do, don't _____ my mistake to the boss!
(A) mention
(B) patent
(C) portray
(D) recognize

_____12. Let's make sure we didn't _____ anything on the list.
(A) irritate
(B) overlook
(C) instruct
(D) reflect

TIME
Basic Words 888

動詞

Chapter 7

457~540

共
300
字

動詞 共 300 字 (457~540)

- □ request 要求
- □ resemble 類似，相似
- □ resolve 解決
- □ respond 回應
- □ restore 恢復
- □ restrain 制止
- □ reunite 團圓，重聚
- □ reveal 揭露，顯示
- □ revolutionize 引起革命
- □ risk 冒險
- □ rot 腐敗
- □ rotate 旋轉
- □ ruin 毀壞
- □ rumor 謠傳，傳說
- □ run into 碰到，不期而遇
- □ rush 衝；催促
- ■ score 得分
- □ scramble 搶，爭奪
- □ scrub 擦洗，刷洗
- □ seize 緊抓
- □ set aside 存，保留
- □ settle 定居
- □ settle for 勉強接受
- □ shatter 粉碎
- □ shrink 縮小
- □ shrug 聳肩
- □ sip 小口啜飲
- □ slay 宰殺
- □ smell 有味道，發臭
- □ snap 折斷
- □ soar 高漲；翱翔
- □ solve 解決
- □ spark 點燃
- □ specialize 專攻，專長於
- □ spit 吐
- □ split 分手
- □ sponsor 贊助
- □ spot 發現
- □ stabilize 使穩定，使固定
- □ stare 盯，凝視
- □ steal 偷竊
- □ stick 固定於；忠於
- □ stimulate 刺激
- □ sting 刺，螫
- □ stink 發出惡臭
- □ strip 剝
- □ struggle 掙扎
- □ stuff 塞入，填入
- □ suffer 患…病；遭受…之苦
- □ suppress 壓制
- □ surf 衝浪
- □ surpass 超越
- □ survive 經歷過…後還活著；生存
- □ switch 轉變
- □ symbolize 象徵

- take on　承擔
- tangle　糾結
- tease　取笑；逗
- tempt　引誘
- tend　傾向於
- terminate　終結，終止
- testify　作證
- thrive　興盛
- torture　折磨
- track down　追蹤到
- trade　交換
- transfer　移轉
- transform　改造
- translate　翻譯
- transmit　傳送，傳導
- transport　運送
- trap　捕捉，困住
- tune in　收聽，收看
- unveil　首度發表
- urge　催促
- vibrate　振動
- vomit　嘔吐
- wander　徘徊，閒逛
- wear off　慢慢消失
- whisper　耳語，說悄悄話
- withhold　隱瞞
- withstand　禁得起；抵擋
- wrap　包，圍

- yell　大聲喊叫

A
B
C
D
E
F
G
H
I
J
K
L
M

□[457] **request** [rɪ`kwɛst] (v.) 要求

Many listeners called to request Ricky Martin songs.
許多聽眾打電話來要求點播瑞奇馬汀的歌。

□[458] **resemble** [rɪ`zɛmbl] (v.) 類似，相似

The model resembles the real house in every detail.
這個模型和真正的房子在每一個細節上都相似。

◆□[459] **resolve** [rɪ`zɑlv] (v.) 解決

Jane asked me to help her resolve a fight between her and her boyfriend.
珍要我幫她解決她和男朋友間的爭端。

□[460] **respond** [rɪ`spɑnd] (v.) 回應

Many countries responded to Taiwan's call for help after the earthquake.
在地震之後，許多國家對台灣的救援要求做出回應。

| request | resemble | resolve | respond |

□⁴⁶¹ **restore** [rɪ`stor] (v.) 恢復

After the operation, his health was quickly restored.
開刀後，他的健康很快就恢復了。

◆□⁴⁶² **restrain** [rɪ`stren] (v.) 制止

The man was fighting with the police and had to be restrained.
當時那個人和警察打鬥，必須加以制止。

□⁴⁶³ **reunite** [ˌrijuˋnaɪt] (v.) 重聚，團圓

She and her husband were finally reunited after 20 years of separation.
在分離二十年之後，她與先生終於破鏡重圓。

◆□⁴⁶⁴ **reveal** [rɪ`vil] (v.) 揭露，顯示

A person's handwriting might reveal a lot about his/her personality.
一個人的筆跡有可能透露出很多他／她的個性。

N
O
P
Q
R
S
T
U
V
W
X
Y
Z

| restore | restrain | reunite | reveal |

A
B
C
D
E
F
G
H
I
J
K
L
M

□⁴⁶⁵ **revolutionize** [ˌrɛvəˈluʃənˌaɪz] (v.) 引起革命

The personal computer revolutionized the computer industry.
個人電腦掀起了電腦業的革命。

□⁴⁶⁶ **risk** [rɪsk] (v.) 冒險

If I take too many days off, I might risk losing my job.
若是我請太多假就要冒丟掉工作的風險。

◆□⁴⁶⁷ **rot** [rɑt] (v.) 腐敗

Put that meat in the refrigerator or it will rot.
將那塊肉放進冰箱，不然它會腐壞。

◆□⁴⁶⁸ **rotate** [ˈrotet] (v.) 旋轉

The Earth rotates on its axis.
地球繞著它的軸心旋轉。

| revolutionize | risk | rot | rotate |

□ 469 **ruin** [ˋruɪn] (v.) 毀壞

Anna's bad mood ruined our romantic weekend.

安娜的壞心情毀了我們的浪漫週末。

□ 470 **rumor** [ˋrumɚ] (v.) 謠傳，傳說

It is rumored that the mayor once had an affair with that TV actress.

謠傳市長曾和那名電視女星有染。

□ 471 **run into** [rʌn ˋɪntu] (v.) 碰到，不期而遇

I ran into an old friend in the shopping mall today.

今天我在購物商場碰見一個老友。

□ 472 **rush** [rʌʃ] (v.) 衝；催促

He had an accident while he was rushing to school this morning.

他早上趕去上課的時候出了車禍。

A
B
C
D
E
F
G
H
I
J
K
L
M

□⁴⁷³ **score** [skor] (v.) 得分

Michael Jordan used to score more than 30 points every game.
麥可喬丹從前每場比賽得分超過卅分。

◆□⁴⁷⁴ **scramble** [ˋskræmbl] (v.) 搶，爭奪

The birds were scrambling for food on the ground.
鳥兒在地上爭食。

◆□⁴⁷⁵ **scrub** [skrʌb] (v.) 擦洗，刷洗

The maid scrubs the kitchen floor once a week.
女佣每星期刷洗廚房地板一次。

□⁴⁷⁶ **seize** [siz] (v.) 緊抓

Seize the opportunity when you see one.
看到機會就要把握。

| score | scramble | scrub | seize° |

□⁴⁷⁷ **set aside** [sɛt ə`saɪd] (v.) 存，保留

My uncle set aside part of his salary for three years, and then he bought a boat.
我叔叔三年來存下他的部分薪水，然後買了一條船。

□⁴⁷⁸ **settle** [`sɛtl̩] (v.) 定居

Over the centuries, many different cultures have settled in this area.
幾個世紀以來，許多不同的文化都在這個區域定居過。

□⁴⁷⁹ **settle for** [`sɛtl̩ fɔr] (v.) 勉強接受

If there's no more steak left, I'll just have to settle for a hamburger.
如果沒有牛排，我就勉強吃個漢堡。

◆□⁴⁸⁰ **shatter** [`ʃætə] (v.) 粉碎

My dreams of becoming a politician were shattered after the revolution.
我的從政之夢在這場革命後粉碎了。

| set aside | settle | settle for | shatter |

◆□⁴⁸¹ **shrink** [ʃrɪŋk] (v.) 縮小

My sweater shrank after I put it in the dryer.
我的毛衣放入烘乾機後就縮水了。

◆□⁴⁸² **shrug** [ʃrʌg] (v.) 聳肩

When you shrug your shoulders, you show
people that you don't care.
你聳肩時就是表示你不在乎。

◆□⁴⁸³ **sip** [sɪp] (v.) 小口啜飲

I like to sip Oolong tea while I work.
我工作時喜歡啜飲烏龍茶。

◆□⁴⁸⁴ **slay** [sle] (v.) 宰殺

My kid brother loves to play those video
games in which he can slay monsters.
我弟弟喜歡玩可以殺怪物的電玩遊戲。

| shrink | shrug | sip | slay |

□[485] **smell** [smɛl] (v.) 有味道，發臭

Your pile of clothes is beginning to smell.
你那堆衣服已經開始發臭了。

◆□[486] **snap** [snæp] (v.) 折斷

You can easily snap one chopstick, but a handful of chopsticks is another story.
一支筷子很容易折斷，但是一把筷子就另當別論了。

◆□[487] **soar** [sor] (v.) 高漲；翱翔

Many believe stock prices will soar after Taiwan joins the WTO.
許多人相信，台灣加入世界貿易組織之後股價會高漲。

□[488] **solve** [sɑlv] (v.) 解決

I can't solve this problem by myself. I need your help.
我自己無法解決這個問題，需要你幫忙。

| smell | snap | soar | solve |

◆□⁴⁸⁹ **spark** [spɑrk] (v.) 點燃

If you don't put out that cigarette before you throw it away here, you might spark a forest fire. 如果你不熄掉香菸就把它丟在這裡，可能會引燃森林大火。

□⁴⁹⁰ **specialize** [ˈspɛʃə͵laɪz] (v.) 專攻，專長於

Our company specializes in making semiconductors.
我們公司以製造半導體見長。

◆□⁴⁹¹ **spit** [spɪt] (v.) 吐

The milk was rotten, so I spit it out.
牛奶壞了，所以我把它吐掉。

□⁴⁹² **split** [splɪt] (v.) 分手

The woman split with her husband because he refused to do any housework.
這個女人和她丈夫分手，因為他完全不肯做家事。

| spark | specialize | spit | split |

□ 493 **sponsor** [ˈspɑnsɚ] (v.) 贊助

Our company is going to sponsor a fund-raising dinner next week.
我們公司將在下週贊助一場募款餐會。

□ 494 **spot** [spɑt] (v.) 發現

The police spotted the runaway suspect on Highway five.
警察在第五公路上發現逃逸的嫌犯。

□ 495 **stabilize** [ˈstebḷˌaɪz] (v.) 使穩定，使固定

A steady supply of products serves to stabilize the market.
供貨平穩可以穩定市場。

◆ □ 496 **stare** [stɛr] (v.) 盯，凝視

That girl was so beautiful that I couldn't stop staring at her.
那個女孩如此美麗，我無法不盯著她看。

| sponsor | spot | stabilize | stare |

A
B
C
D
E
F
G
H
I
J
K
L
M

□⁴⁹⁷ **steal** [stil] (v.) 偷竊

The thief stole many expensive things from my apartment.
小偷從我家偷走許多值錢的東西。

□⁴⁹⁸ **stick** [stɪk] (v.) 固定於；忠於

When giving a speech, remember to stick to one topic.
演講時記得要固定一個主題。

□⁴⁹⁹ **stimulate** [ˋstɪmjə,let] (v.) 刺激

Advertising stimulates people to buy.
廣告刺激人們消費。

◆□⁵⁰⁰ **sting** [stɪŋ] (v.) 刺，螫

If you stay very still, the bee probably won't sting you.
如果你靜止不動，蜜蜂可能就不會叮你。

| steal | stick | stimulate | sting |

N
O
P
Q
R

T
U
V
W
X
Y
Z

◆ □⁵⁰¹ **stink** [stɪŋk] (v.) 發出惡臭

The spoiled food in the refrigerator stinks.
冰箱裡腐敗的食物臭死了。

◆ □⁵⁰² **strip** [strɪp] (v.) 剝

It took hours to strip the old wallpaper off of grandma's walls!
剝除祖母牆上的舊壁紙，花了好幾小時的工夫。

□⁵⁰³ **struggle** [ˋstrʌgl] (v.) 掙扎

I always struggle to get to work on time.
每天為了準時上班我都得掙扎一番。

□⁵⁰⁴ **stuff** [stʌf] (v.) 塞入，填入

He stuffed old clothes into the bag.
他將舊衣服塞入袋子中。

A
B
C
D
E
F
G
H
I
J
K
L
M

□⁵⁰⁵ **suffer** [ˈsʌfə] (v.) 患…病；遭受…之苦

He's been suffering from a severe memory loss since the car accident.
在車禍後，他就患了嚴重的失憶症。

◆□⁵⁰⁶ **suppress** [səˈprɛs] (v.) 壓制

Tell me how you really feel—you shouldn't suppress your feelings.
告訴我你真正的感覺——你不應該壓抑你的情感。

□⁵⁰⁷ **surf** [sɝf] (v.) 衝浪

People from Australia love to surf on the weekends.
澳洲人喜歡在週末衝浪。

□⁵⁰⁸ **surpass** [səˈpæs] (v.) 超越

The money we collected for the charity has surpassed our goal.
我們募集的慈善捐款已經超越了目標。

□⁵⁰⁹ **survive** [sə`vaɪv] (v.) 經歷過…後還活著；生存

My father survived two wars, three floods and four earthquakes.
我父親經歷兩次戰爭、三次洪水與四次地震都依然健在。

□⁵¹⁰ **switch** [swɪtʃ] (v.) 轉變

Most people have switched from using typewriters to using computers.
大多數人已經由使用打字機，改為用電腦。

□⁵¹¹ **symbolize** [`sɪmbḷ͵aɪz] (v.) 象徵

What do you think this painting is supposed to symbolize?
你認為這幅畫是在象徵什麼？

□⁵¹² **take on** [tek ɑn] (v.) 承擔

I'm too busy—there's no way I can take on any more work.
我太忙了，絕對無法承擔更多工作。

◆□⁵¹³ **tangle** [ˈtæŋgl] (v.) 糾結

The cat has tangled my wool.
那隻貓把我的毛線弄得一團亂。

□⁵¹⁴ **tease** [tiz] (v.) 取笑；逗

Nobody likes to be teased.
沒有人喜歡被取笑。

◆□⁵¹⁵ **tempt** [tɛmpt] (v.) 引誘

That company is tempting me with a great job offer.
那家公司以很好的工作機會引誘我。

□⁵¹⁶ **tend** [tɛnd] (v.) 傾向於

I tend to enjoy indoor activities more than outdoor ones.
我比較偏好室內活動而非戶外活動。

| tangle | tease | tempt | tend |

□[517] **terminate** [ˋtɝmə͵net] (v.) 終結，終止

Your contract has been terminated.
你的合約已經被終止了。

□[518] **testify** [ˋtɛstə͵faɪ] (v.) 作證

Many people testified in court that the police arrested the wrong person.
許多人在法庭上作證說警察抓錯人。

◆□[519] **thrive** [θraɪv] (v.) 興盛

Business thrived after we hired a new sales clerk.
我們雇用新售貨員後，生意興盛起來。

□[520] **torture** [ˋtɔrtʃɚ] (v.) 折磨

Some victims of the fire are tortured by painful memories.
這場火災的一些受害者受著痛苦回憶的折磨。

| terminate | testify | thrive | torture |

A

B

C

D

E

F

G

H

I

J

K

L

M

□ [521] **track down** [træk daʊn] (v.) 追蹤到

We need to see if we can track down the owner of this car.
我們要看是否能追蹤到車主。

□ [522] **trade** [tred] (v.) 交換

I'll trade you my bicycle for your in-line skates!
我用腳踏車跟你換直排輪鞋！

□ [523] **transfer** [træns`fɜ] (v.) 移轉

Transfer the file to this disk and then give it to Pamela.
將這個檔案轉入磁碟片後再交給潘蜜拉。

□ [524] **transform** [træns`fɔrm] (v.) 改造

The Internet has transformed the business world.
網際網路已經改造了商業界。

| track down | trade | transfer | transform |

□⁵²⁵ **translate** [træns`let] (v.) 翻譯

My job is to translate English articles into Chinese.
我的工作是將英文文章翻譯成中文。

◆□⁵²⁶ **transmit** [træns`mɪt] (v.) 傳送，傳導

Sound waves can be transmitted through water.
水可以傳導聲波。

□⁵²⁷ **transport** [træns`pɔrt] (v.) 運送

It always takes several months to transport items by boat.
透過船運運送貨物總要耗時數月。

□⁵²⁸ **trap** [træp] (v.) 捕捉，困住

The snowstorm trapped thousands of skiers on the mountain.
這場暴風雪把數千名滑雪者困在山上。

N O P Q R S T U V W X Y Z

| translate | transmit | transport | trap |

動詞

□[529] **tune in** [tjun ɪn] (v.) 收聽，收看

If I want to know how the show ends, I'll have to tune in again tomorrow.
我如果想要知道這個節目的結局，明天還得繼續收看。

□[530] **unveil** [ʌn`vel] (v.) 首度發表

The rock star will unveil his new song at his concert tonight.
這位搖滾巨星將在今晚的演唱會上發表他的新歌。

□[531] **urge** [ɜdʒ] (v.) 催促

The salesman kept on urging me to buy the car today.
業務員一直催促我今天買車。

□[532] **vibrate** [`vaɪbret] (v.) 振動

My cell phone vibrates when I get a call.
我的手機在來電時會振動。

| tune in | unveil | urge | vibrate |

□ 533 **vomit** [ˋvɑmɪt] (v.) 嘔吐

I got sick on the boat and vomited on the deck.
我暈船了，並在甲板上嘔吐。

□ 534 **wander** [ˋwɑndɚ] (v.) 徘徊，閒逛

Having forgotten where he parked his car, John wandered around the parking lot for hours. 約翰在停車場徘徊了好幾個小時，因為他忘記他的車子停在哪裡了。

□ 535 **wear off** [wɛr ɔf] (v.) 慢慢消失

When will the effects of this medicine wear off?
這個藥的藥效什麼時候會退？

□ 536 **whisper** [ˋhwɪspɚ] (v.) 耳語，說悄悄話

Please whisper so that others won't hear.
請低聲說話才不會讓別人聽到。

動詞

◆□537 **withhold** [wɪθˋhold] (v.) 隱瞞

He tried to withhold the truth from us.
他企圖對我們隱瞞真相。

◆□538 **withstand** [wɪðˋstænd] (v.) 禁得起；抵擋

His work of art will undoubtedly withstand the test of time.
他的藝術作品無疑地可以禁得起時間的考驗。

◆□539 **wrap** [ræp] (v.) 包，圍

Wrap this shawl round your shoulders.It's cold out there.
外面很冷，把這個披肩圍在肩膀上吧。

□540 **yell** [jɛl] (v.) 大聲喊叫

I can't bear it when a bar is so noisy that you have to yell to make yourself heard.
我受不了酒吧很吵而必須大喊才能讓別人聽到自己說的話。

| withhold | withstand | wrap | yell |

解答請見 p. 290

_____ 1. This new video phone will _____ the
way we communicate.
(A) solve
(B) revolutionize
(C) whisper
(D) thrive

_____ 2. Guess who I _____ at the supermarket.
(A) stuck to
(B) took on
(C) ran into
(D) wore off

_____ 3. It took me an hour to _____ the kitchen
and living room floors.
(A) scrub
(B) resemble
(C) rotate
(D) stabilize

_____ 4. Are you sure you can _____ all that into
your suitcase?
(A) surpass
(B) trap
(C) withstand
(D) stuff

_____ 5. The host reminded everyone to_____ to next week's show.
(A) tune in
(B) track down
(C) set aside
(D) settle for

_____ 6. We're looking for someone to _____ our brochure into French.
(A) reunite
(B) scramble
(C) translate
(D) specialize

_____ 7. The old woman _____ her tea as she watched TV.
(A) rushed
(B) sipped
(C) resolved
(D) sparked

_____ 8. Beer companies like to _____ sporting events.
(A) tempt
(B) suppress
(C) transmit
(D) sponsor

_____ 9. As I walked through the forest, a twig
_____ beneath my feet.
(A) snapped
(B) switched
(C) transferred
(D) wandered

_____10. The police quickly moved in to _____
order in the neighborhood.
(A) struggle
(B) unveil
(C) transform
(D) restore

_____11. Why does the kitchen _____ so badly?
(A) tease
(B) risk
(C) stink
(D) ruin

_____12. See if you can _____ anything wrong at
the factory.
(A) spot
(B) reveal
(C) settle
(D) stare

TIME

Basic Words 888

名詞

Chapter 8

541~628

共 348 字

■ accent 口音，腔調

□ access 管道

□ acclaim 讚賞，喝采

□ accomplishment 成就

□ addition 新增的人或東西

□ address 演說

□ advantage 優勢，優點

□ adviser 顧問；指導老師（教授）

□ affair 婚外情；事務

□ aftermath 餘波，後果

□ aisle 通道

□ album 專輯

□ alien 外國人；外星人

□ ambition 抱負；野心

□ ancestor 祖先

□ angle 角度

□ appreciation 欣賞；感激

□ approval 批准，許可

□ argument 爭論；理由

□ ashes 骨灰

□ assignment 指定作業，功課

□ astrology 占星術（學）

□ astronomy 天文學

□ auction 拍賣

□ availability 可取得；便利

□ award 獎

■ backpack 背包

□ balance 平衡

□ barbarian 野蠻人

□ behavior 行為

□ benefit 利益，好處

□ billion 十億

□ biography 傳記

□ blade 刀片

□ blanket 毛毯

□ blood pressure 血壓

□ blueprint 藍圖；計畫

□ blunder 大錯

□ boast 誇口

□ brake 煞車

□ breakthrough 突破

□ brick 磚

□ brutality 殘忍；野蠻行為

□ budget 預算

□ bully 欺凌弱小的人

■ career 生涯

□ category 種類

□ celebrity 名人

□ CEO 總裁（是 Chief Executive Officer 的縮寫）

□ championship 冠軍賽

□ channel 頻道

□ chaos 混亂

□ character 角色，人物

□ charm 魅力，吸引力

□ chart 排行榜；圖表
□ chunk 大塊
□ circulation 循環
□ classic 經典作品
□ client 客戶，顧客
□ climate 氣候
□ climax 頂點，最高潮
□ clinic 診所
□ clue 線索
□ cluster 群；（花、果實等的）束
□ coach 教練，指導者
□ collector 收藏家
□ comeback 東山再起，復出
□ comic strip 連環漫畫
□ commercial 廣告片
□ competition 競賽
□ competitiveness 競爭性
□ competitor 競爭者
□ compliment 讚美
□ concentration 集中，專注
□ concept 觀念
□ conflict 衝突
□ conscience 良心，良知
□ construction 建造
□ consultant 顧問
□ consumption 消耗量，消費
□ contest 比賽

□ contestant 參賽者，角逐者
□ controversy 爭議
□ copyright 版權
□ cosmetic 化妝品
□ course 路線，方向
□ court 球場
□ critic 批評者

B
C
D
E
F
G
H
I
J
K
L
M

□⁵⁴¹ **accent** [ˋæksɛnt] (n.) 口音，腔調
Southern U.S. accents are very pleasing to the ear.
美國南方口音非常悅耳。

□⁵⁴² **access** [ˋæksɛs] (n.) 管道
Do you have access to students' personal files?
你有管道可以取得學生個人資料嗎？

◆□⁵⁴³ **acclaim** [əˋklem] (n.) 讚賞，喝采
His new book on dog care has received much acclaim.
他所寫的關於養狗的新書得到許多讚賞。

□⁵⁴⁴ **accomplishment** [əˋkamplɪʃmənt] (n.) 成就
Dr. David Ho is widely respected for his accomplishments in AIDS research.
何大一博士因為在愛滋病研究方面的成就廣受敬重。

□ 545 **addition** [əˋdɪʃən] (n.) 新增的人或東西

This is Sally—she's a new addition to our company.
這位是莎莉——她是本公司的新進員工。

□ 546 **address** [əˋdrɛs] (n.) 演說

The president's address was shown on all the major TV stations.
總統的演說在所有主要電視台播放。

□ 547 **advantage** [ədˋvæntɪdʒ] (n.) 優勢，優點

He has an advantage over me because the teacher is his mom.
他比我占有優勢，因為老師是他媽媽。

□ 548 **adviser** [ədˋvaɪzə] (n.) 顧問；指導老師（教授）

The advisers to the President have a lot of responsibility.
總統的顧問有許多責任。

N O P Q R S T U V W X Y Z

addition　　address　　advantage　　adviser

B
C
D
E
F
G
H
I
J
K
L
M

☐⁵⁴⁹ **affair** [əˋfɛr] (n.) 婚外情；事務

When he found out about his wife's affair he asked for a divorce.
他發現妻子的婚外情後要求離婚。

◆☐⁵⁵⁰ **aftermath** [ˋæftɚ͵mæθ] (n.) 餘波，後果

People are trying to get back to normal life in the aftermath of war.
在戰爭的餘波中，人們設法回復正常生活。

☐⁵⁵¹ **aisle** [aɪl] (n.) 通道

Whould you like a window seat or an aisle seat?
您想要靠窗的座位還是靠走道的座位呢？

☐⁵⁵² **album** [ˋælbəm] (n.) 專輯

I have over 100 rock and roll albums.
我收藏了超過一百張的搖滾樂專輯。

□⁵⁵³ **alien** [ˈelɪən] (n.) 外國人;外星人

You'll be an alien during your stay in the US.
你在美國期間就是外國人。

□⁵⁵⁴ **ambition** [æmˋbɪʃən] (n.) 抱負;野心

My father has always encouraged me to
pursue my ambitions.
我父親總是一直鼓勵我追求自己的抱負。

□⁵⁵⁵ **ancestor** [ˈænsɛstə] (n.) 祖先

My ancestors came to Taiwan from Canton.
我的祖先從廣東來到台灣。

□⁵⁵⁶ **angle** [ˈæŋgl] (n.) 角度

You can approach this problem from many
different angles.
你可以從許多不同的角度探討這個問題。

B
C
D
E
F
G
H
I
J
K
L
M

□⁵⁵⁷ **appreciation** [ə͵priʃɪ`eʃən] (n.) 欣賞；感激

His boss gave him a raise, out of appreciation for his excellent work.
他老闆因為很欣賞他傑出的工作表現，而為他加了薪。

□⁵⁵⁸ **approval** [ə`pruvl] (n.) 批准，許可

We need to get the boss's approval before we can start this new project.
開始這項新的計畫之前，我們需要獲得老闆的許可。

□⁵⁵⁹ **argument** [`ɑrgjəmənt] (n.) 爭論；理由

I got into a huge argument with my big brother last night.
昨晚我與哥哥發生激烈的爭論。

□⁵⁶⁰ **ashes** [`æʃɪz] (n.) 骨灰

I keep the ashes of my late grandfather in this urn.
我將已故祖父的骨灰存放在這個甕裡。

□ 561 **assignment** [ə`saɪnmənt] (n.) 指定作業，功課

It took me over six hours to complete today's assignment.
我花了六個多小時才完成今天的作業。

□ 562 **astrology** [ə`strɑlədʒɪ] (n.) 占星術（學）

The Babylonians used astrology to predict war, famine and weather as well.
巴比倫人用占星術來預測戰爭、饑荒以及天氣。

□ 563 **astronomy** [ə`strɑnəmɪ] (n.) 天文學

Astronomy is the scientific study of the universe.
天文學是一門研究宇宙的科學。

◆□ 564 **auction** [`ɔkʃən] (n.) 拍賣

Princess Diana's personal letters will be sold at the next auction.
黛安娜王妃的私人信件將在下一場拍賣中出售。

N
O
P
Q
R
S
T
U
V
W
X
Y
Z

□565 **availability** [ə,velə`bɪlətɪ] (n.) 可取得；便利

Many people blame the high murder rates in the US on the easy availability of guns there.
美國兇殺案比例高，許多人說是因為槍枝太容易取得。

□566 **award** [ə`wɔrd] (n.) 獎

He received an award for his volunteer work after the 921 Earthquake.
他因為在九二一大地震後擔任義工而獲獎。

□567 **backpack** [`bæk,pæk] (n.) 背包

I left my backpack on the train.
我把背包遺忘在火車上了。

□568 **balance** [`bæləns] (n.) 平衡

Dancers need to have great balance.
舞者需要有很好的平衡感。

□⁵⁶⁹ **barbarian** [bɑrˋbɛrɪən] (n.) 野蠻人

Only barbarians solve problems with fists.
只有野蠻人才用拳頭解決問題。

□⁵⁷⁰ **behavior** [bɪˋhevjə] (n.) 行為

You've always on your best behavior when you're with your uncle.
你和你叔叔在一起時，總是表現的最好。

□⁵⁷¹ **benefit** [ˋbɛnəfɪt] (n.) 利益，好處

The benefits you can get from exercise are priceless.
你得自運動的好處是無價的。

□⁵⁷² **billion** [ˋbɪljən] (n.) 十億

There are more than six billion people on our planet.
我們的星球上有超過六十億的人。

barbarian | behavior | benefit | billion

名詞

□⁵⁷³ **biography** [baɪˋɑɡrəfɪ] (n.) 傳記

I like reading biographies of famous people.
我喜歡閱讀名人傳記。

◆□⁵⁷⁴ **blade** [bled] (n.) 刀片

The blade on my razor is dull and it needs to be replaced.
我的刮鬍刀刀片鈍了，要換掉。

□⁵⁷⁵ **blanket** [ˋblæŋkɪt] (n.) 毛毯

It's cold tonight—you'd better take an extra blanket.
今晚很冷——你最好多拿件毛毯。

□⁵⁷⁶ **blood pressure** [ˋblʌd͵prɛʃɚ] (n.) 血壓

Arguing with you makes my blood pressure go up.
和你爭論使我血壓升高。

| biography | blade | blanket | blood pressure |

□⁵⁷⁷ **blueprint** [`blu`prɪnt] (n.) 藍圖；計畫

The blueprints for this building are not very accurate.
這棟建築的藍圖並不是很精確。

◆ □⁵⁷⁸ **blunder** [`blʌndɚ] (n.) 大錯

The girl's death caused by a hospital's blunder is under investigation.
醫院的大錯造成那名女孩的死亡事件正被調查中。

□⁵⁷⁹ **boast** [bost] (n.) 誇口

The medals he won are his constant boasts.
他常常吹噓他所贏得的獎牌。

□⁵⁸⁰ **brake** [brek] (n.) 煞車

The taxi driver suddenly applied his brakes.
計程車司機突然踩煞車。

| blueprint | blunder | boast | brake |

名詞

□581 **breakthrough** [`brek,θru] (n.) 突破

Scientists have made a breakthrough in the treatment of AIDS.
科學家在治療愛滋病方面有了突破。

□582 **brick** [brɪk] (n.) 磚

This building is made completely of bricks.
這棟建築物完全是磚造的。

□583 **brutality** [bru`tælətɪ] (n.) 殘忍；野蠻行為

If you've never been through war, you can't imagine the brutality.
如果你沒經歷過戰爭，你無法想像有多殘忍。

□584 **budget** [`bʌdʒɪt] (n.) 預算

These days, you can't make a good movie on a small budget.
這年頭，小預算拍不出好電影。

| breakthrough | brick | brutality | budget |

◆□⁵⁸⁵ **bully** [ˋbulɪ] (n.) 欺凌弱小的人

This story is about a boy who gets into a fight with a bully.

這是關於一個男孩與一個惡霸爭鬥的故事。

□⁵⁸⁶ **career** [kəˋrɪr] (n.) 生涯

She wants to develop her career before she marries.

她想要在結婚前拓展她的事業。

□⁵⁸⁷ **category** [ˋkætə͵gorɪ] (n.) 種類

The voters fall into three main categories: KMT, DPP and New Party.

選民有三大類：國民黨、民進黨和新黨。

□⁵⁸⁸ **celebrity** [səˋlɛbrətɪ] (n.) 名人

Celebrities who live in Beverly Hills often dine at our restaurant.

住在比佛利山莊的名人們經常在我們餐廳用餐。

| bully | career | category | celebrity |

名詞

□589 **CEO** (n.) 總裁（是 Chief Executive Officer 的縮寫）

My goal is to become the CEO of my company.
我的目標是成為公司的總裁。

□590 **championship** [ˈtʃæmpɪənˌʃɪp] (n.) 冠軍賽

Only two teams will compete in the championship.
只有兩個隊伍可以參加冠軍賽。

□591 **channel** [ˈtʃænl] (n.) 頻道

We get 108 channels on our television.
我們的電視有一百零八個頻道。

□592 **chaos** [ˈkeɑs] (n.) 混亂

There was chaos everywhere after the earthquake.
地震發生後到處都很混亂。

□⁵⁹³ **character** [ˋkærɪktə] (n.) 角色，人物

There're so many characters in *War and Peace* that sometimes you forget who's who.
《戰爭與和平》裡的人物太多了，有時會忘記誰是誰。

□⁵⁹⁴ **charm** [tʃɑrm] (n.) 魅力，吸引力

He's got a lot of charm. No wonder he has so many girlfriends.
他真的很有魅力。難怪他有這麼多女朋友。

□⁵⁹⁵ **chart** [tʃɑrt] (n.) 排行榜；圖表

Charlotte Church's latest song is at the top of the singles chart.
夏綠蒂的最新歌曲是單曲排行榜冠軍。

◆□⁵⁹⁶ **chunk** [tʃʌŋk] (n.) 大塊

I love it when there are large chunks of chocolate in my chocolate chip cookies.
我喜歡在巧克力碎片餅乾中吃到大塊的巧克力。

N O P Q R S T U V W X Y Z

| character | charm | chart | chunk |

名詞

□⁵⁹⁷ **circulation** [ˌsɝkjəˋleʃən] (n.) 循環

A little drink will stimulate your circulation and warm you up.
喝點酒可以刺激你的血液循環，讓你感覺暖和。

□⁵⁹⁸ **classic** [ˋklæsɪk] (n.) 經典作品

I used to love reading the classics, like *A Tale of Two Cities*.
我以前最愛讀經典作品，像是《雙城記》。

□⁵⁹⁹ **client** [ˋklaɪənt] (n.) 客戶，顧客

I have a meeting with an important client on Friday.
星期五我與一個重要的客戶有約。

□⁶⁰⁰ **climate** [ˋklaɪmɪt] (n.) 氣候

People love San Francisco for its mild climate.
舊金山因為氣候溫和受人喜愛。

| circulation | classic | client | climate |

□ 601 **climax** [ˋklaɪmæks] (n.) 頂點，最高潮

The climax of the movie wasn't very exciting.
這部電影的高潮並不刺激。

□ 602 **clinic** [ˋklɪnɪk] (n.) 診所

I had a toothache, so I went to the dental clinic to see the dentist.
我牙痛，所以到牙科診所去看牙醫。

□ 603 **clue** [klu] (n.) 線索

The police couldn't find any clues at the murder scene.
警方在犯罪現場找不到任何線索。

◆□ 604 **cluster** [ˋklʌstə] (n.) 群；（花、果實等的）束

You can find a cluster of bookstores near the university.
在大學附近書店林立。

climax   clinic   clue   cluster

□[605] **coach** [kotʃ] (n.) 教練，指導者

I really like my baseball coach. He's the reason our team is so successful.
我非常喜歡我的棒球教練。他是我們這支隊伍如此成功的原因。

□[606] **collector** [kəˋlɛktə] (n.) 收藏家

My grandfather has been a stamp collector all his life.
我祖父一輩子都是郵票收藏家。

◆□[607] **comeback** [ˋkʌm,bæk] (n.) 東山再起，復出

There's still time for us to make a comeback.
我們還有時間東山再起。

□[608] **comic strip** [ˋkɑmɪk ˋstrɪp] (n.) 連環漫畫

Garfield is my favorite comic strip.
《加菲貓》是我最喜愛的連環漫畫。

| coach | collector | comeback | comic strip |

☐⁶⁰⁹ **commercial** [kə`mɝʃəl] (n.) 廣告片

I can't get that SKII commercial out of my head—Take a closer look....
我對 SKII 的那支廣告印象深刻──再靠近一點
……。

☐⁶¹⁰ **competition** [ˌkɑmpə`tɪʃən] (n.) 競賽

A thousand people took part in the chess competition.
有一千人參加這場西洋棋比賽。

☐⁶¹¹ **competitiveness** [kəm`pɛtətɪvnɪs] (n.) 競爭性

She doesn't like the competitiveness of team sports.
她不喜歡團隊運動的那種競爭性。

☐⁶¹² **competitor** [kəm`pɛtətə] (n.) 競爭者

It's hard for his bookstore to make money because there are too many competitors around.
他的書店很難賺錢，因為附近有太多競爭者。

commercial | competition | competitiveness | competitor

名詞

◆□ 613 **compliment** [ˋkɑmpləmənt] (n.) 讚美

Everyone likes to hear a compliment
人人都喜歡聽到讚美。

□ 614 **concentration** [ˌkɑnsṇˋtreʃən] (n.) 集中，專注

You need to have good concentration to
play a musical instrument.
你演奏樂器時必須十分專注。

□ 615 **concept** [ˋkɑnsɛpt] (n.) 觀念

This is a difficult mathematical concept to
understand.
這是一個很難理解的數學觀念。

□ 616 **conflict** [ˋkɑnflɪkt] (n.) 衝突

Coming from different backgrounds, the
young couple had many conflicts
由於來自不同的背景，這對年輕夫婦發生許多衝
突。

◆□⁶¹⁷ **conscience** [ˋkɑnʃəns] (n.) 良心，良知

After I lied to my mother, I had a quilty conscience all day.
我對母親撒謊之後整天良心不安。

□⁶¹⁸ **construction** [kənˋstrʌkʃən] (n.) 建造

This construction will cost more money than we expected.
這項營造工程耗資將會比我們原先預估的高。

◆□⁶¹⁹ **consultant** [kənˋsʌltənt] (n.) 顧問

He works as a consultant for large trading companies.
他身為幾家大貿易公司的顧問。

◆□⁶²⁰ **consumption** [kənˋsʌmpʃən] (n.) 消耗量，消費

Consumption of Coke has increased this year in Taiwan.
台灣今年的可樂消耗量增加。

conscience | construction | consultant | consumption

A

B

C

D

E

F

G

H

I

J

K

L

M

□⁶²¹ **contest** [ˋkɑntɛst] (n.) 比賽

If I win the contest, I'll take a trip to Hawaii.
如果贏得這場比賽，我將前往夏威夷旅行。

◆□⁶²² **contestant** [kənˋtɛstənt] (n.) 參賽者，角逐者

Two weeks ago one of the contestants answered every question correctly.
兩星期前一名參賽者答對了所有的問題。

□⁶²³ **controversy** [ˋkɑntrə͵vɝsɪ] (n.) 爭議

The controversy over the new rule will soon be over.
對於新規定的爭議將會很快結束。

□⁶²⁴ **copyright** [ˋkɑpɪ͵raɪt] (n.) 版權

Our magazine has copyright to all the articles.
我們雜誌擁有所有文章的版權。

| contest | contestant | controversy | copyright |

□ 625 **cosmetic** [kɑz`mɛtɪk] (n.) 化妝品

Japanese women spend a lot of money on cosmetics.
日本女性花很多錢買化妝品。

□ 626 **course** [kors] (n.) 路線，方向

The typhoon has taken a new course and is moving towards Japan.
颱風路線改變，直撲日本。

□ 627 **court** [kort] (n.) 球場

Our school is going to build a new basketball court.
我們學校將要興建一座新的籃球場。

◆□ 628 **critic** [`krɪtɪk] (n.) 批評者

Critics said that the pianist lacks real talent.
評論家說這位鋼琴家缺乏真正的天賦。

| cosmetic | course | court | critic |

解答請見 p. 290

_____ 1. The government's weather bureau tracked the _____ of the big typhoon.
(A) aisle
(B) course
(C) bully
(D) concept

_____ 2. A talented writer, Lisa has won many _____ for her short stories.
(A) competitors
(B) copyrights
(C) awards
(D) breakthroughs

_____ 3. Ralph stayed up all night finishing his English _____.
(A) assignment
(B) critic
(C) accent
(D) category

_____ 4. Sometimes _____ are shown twice in a row to make people remember them.
(A) channels
(B) contests
(C) affairs
(D) commercials

_____ 5. People say that if you have a strong
_____ to succeed, then you will.
(A) addition
(B) championship
(C) competition
(D) ambition

_____ 6. The boss didn't see the _____ of
spending money on a new computer
system.
(A) boast
(B) balance
(C) benefit
(D) construction

_____ 7. _____followed the politician everywhere
he went.
(A) Controversy
(B) Access
(C) Circulation
(D) Conscience

_____ 8. The basketball team tried to make a
_____ in the second half of the game.
(A) concentration
(B) court
(C) comeback
(D) chaos

_____ 9. Can we complete the project on such a small _____ ?
(A) budget
(B) advantage
(C) climax
(D) consumption

_____10. Mr. Lee was proud of his son's _____ .
(A) cosmetics
(B) accomplishments
(C) conflicts
(D) blankets

_____11. The _____ main purpose was to raise money for charity.
(A) barbarian's
(B) charm's
(C) criticism's
(D) auction's

_____12. In the _____ of the earthquake, people tried hard to resume a normal life.
(A) adviser
(B) angle
(C) aftermath
(D) ancestor

TIME

Basic Words 888

名詞

Chapter 9

629~716

共
348
字

- criticism 評論，批評
- cruise 巡航，漫遊
- culture 文化
- cunning 狡猾，奸詐
- ■ damage 損害
- deadline 截止期限
- debt 債務
- decade 十年
- degree 學位
- despair 絕望
- determination 決心
- device 裝置
- diet 飲食
- direction 說明，指示
- directory 通訊錄；名錄
- discipline 紀律
- disguise 偽裝
- division 部門
- doctorate 博士學位
- drama 戲劇
- durability 耐用性，持久性
- ■ efficiency 效率
- effort 努力
- ego 自我
- emergency 緊急狀況；急診
- emphasis 強調，加重
- enthusiast 熱中者
- environment 環境

- episode 一集
- era 時代，紀元
- essary 文章，短論
- evidence 證據
- executive 高級主管
- exhibit 展覽
- explosive 炸藥
- exposure 暴露
- expression 說法
- ■ factor 因素
- fair 博覽會；市集
- fantasy 幻想
- fate 命運
- fatigue 疲勞，疲倦
- feast 宴會
- feat 壯舉
- feedback 反應；回饋
- festival 節慶
- figure 身材
- fitness 體能狀況
- final 決賽
- flavor 口味
- focus 焦點
- formation 形狀；形成
- formula 配方；公式
- fortune 大筆錢財，財富
- foundation 基金會
- founder 創辦人

□ fraud 騙人的東西；詐欺
□ fusion 融合
■ galaxy 星系，銀河
□ gear 裝備
□ generation 同時代的人；一代
□ germ 細菌
□ glance 一瞥
□ glimpse 一瞥
□ globe 地球；球
□ goal 目標
□ gossip 閒話
□ gourmet 美食家
□ grounds 房屋四周的土地和
　花園
□ guesthouse 賓館
□ guide 指南
■ habitat 動物的棲息地
□ harmony 和諧
□ horizon 地平線
□ host 主持人
■ identification 身分證明
□ illustration 插圖
□ illustrator 插畫家
□ immigrant （移入的）移民
□ impact 衝擊
□ incident 事件；事故
□ individual 個人
□ ingredient 成分

□ injury 傷害
□ inquiry 詢問
□ insecurity 不安全
□ inspiration 啓發，靈感
□ intensity 激烈

□⁶²⁹ **criticism** [ˈkrɪtəˌsɪzəm] (n.) 評論，批評

It is difficult to take criticism from others calmly.
要平靜地接受他人批評很難。

□⁶³⁰ **cruise** [kruz] (n.) 巡航，漫遊

The liner is making a round-the-world cruise this year.
這艘客輪今年在做環球巡航。

□⁶³¹ **culture** [ˈkʌltʃə] (n.) 文化

I went to Spain to study Spanish culture.
我去西班牙研究西班牙文化。

◆□⁶³² **cunning** [ˈkʌnɪŋ] (n.) 狡猾，奸詐

Some cunning may be necessary when you're trying to find out if someone is lying to you.
要查出某人是否在欺騙你，狡猾也許是必須的。

| criticism | cruise | culture | cunning |

N
O
P
Q
R
S
T
U
V
W
X
Y
Z

□ 633 **damage** [ˋdæmɪdʒ] (n.) 損害

The typhoon caused great damage to the little town.
颱風在這個小鎮上造成了很大的損害。

□ 634 **deadline** [ˋdɛd,laɪn] (n.) 截止期限

The teacher says that everyone must hand in the report by the deadline.
老師說每一個人都得在截止期限前把報告交出來。

□ 635 **debt** [dɛt] (n.) 債務

He managed to pay off his debts in two years.
他設法在兩年內還清債務。

□ 636 **decade** [ˋdɛked] (n.) 十年

I've lived in America for more than a decade now.
我已在美國住超過十年了。

| damage | deadline | debt | decade |

名詞

□⁶³⁷ **degree** [dɪˋgri] (n.) 學位

She has two degrees, one in French and one in chemistry.
她擁有法文與化學的雙重學位。

◆□⁶³⁸ **despair** [dɪˋspɛr] (n.) 絕望

A sense of despair at work means you are ready for a vacation.
工作時有絕望的感覺代表你該去度個假了。

□⁶³⁹ **determination** [dɪ,tɜməˋneʃən] (n.) 決心

His determination has impressed his boss.
他的決心令他的老闆印象深刻。

□⁶⁴⁰ **device** [dɪˋvaɪs] (n.) 裝置

I bought a device that will make my stereo system sound better.
我買了一個會讓音響系統聽起來更棒的裝置。

□⁶⁴¹ **diet** [ˋdaɪət] (n.) 飲食

My diet was terrible while I was in college.
我大學時的飲食很糟糕。

□⁶⁴² **direction** [dəˋrɛkʃən] (n.) 說明，指示

We were able to complete our project on time under our boss's direction.
在我們上司的指示下，我們得以準時完成計畫。

□⁶⁴³ **directory** [dəˋrɛktərɪ] (n.) 通訊錄；名錄

I found your phone number in the old church directory.
我在那本舊的教會通訊錄上找到你的電話號碼。

□⁶⁴⁴ **discipline** [ˋdɪsəplɪn] (n.) 紀律

He learned organization and discipline while serving in the army.
他在軍中服役的時候學會了組織與紀律。

| diet | direction | directory | discipline |

名詞

◆□⁶⁴⁵ **disguise** [dɪsˋgaɪz] (n.) 偽裝

The butterfly is protected by its natural disguise—it looks just like a leaf.
這隻蝴蝶受到天然偽裝的保護——牠看起來就像一片樹葉。

□⁶⁴⁶ **division** [dəˋvɪʒən] (n.) 部門

The sales division in our office works long hours.
我們公司的銷售部門工作時間很長。

□⁶⁴⁷ **doctorate** [ˋdɑktərɪt] (n.) 博士學位

My father received his doctorate in 1984.
我父親在一九八四年得到博士學位。

□⁶⁴⁸ **drama** [ˋdrɑmə] (n.) 戲劇

I like watching television dramas. *Dynasty* is my favorite.
我喜歡看電視劇。《朝代》影集是我的最愛。

| disguise | division | doctorate | drama |

◆□⁶⁴⁹ **durability** [ˌdjʊrəˈbɪlətɪ] (n.) 耐用性，持久性

Durability is the most important thing to look for when buying clothes.
購買衣服時，首要注意的是耐用性。

□⁶⁵⁰ **efficiency** [ɪˈfɪʃənsɪ] (n.) 效率

The only thing my boss cares about is efficiency.
我的老闆唯一在乎的是效率。

□⁶⁵¹ **effort** [ˈɛfət] (n.) 努力

I appreciate your effort, but I think I should do this alone.
感謝你的努力，但我想我應該獨自完成這件事。

□⁶⁵² **ego** [ˈigo] (n.) 自我

Artists are often people with big egos.
藝術家常常是自我意識強烈的人。

| durability | efficiency | effort | ego |

名詞

□^653 **emergency** [ɪˋmɝdʒənsɪ] (n.) 緊急狀況；急診

You should call 119 when there's an emergency.
緊急狀況時應打一一九電話。

□^654 **emphasis** [ˋɛmfəsɪs] (n.) 強調，加重

I think we should put as much emphasis on preventing diseases as we do on curing them.
我認為我們應該預防與治療並重。

□^655 **enthusiast** [ɪnˋθjuzɪ͵æst] (n.) 熱中者

He is a real baseball enthusiast.
他真是個棒球愛好者。

□^656 **environment** [ɪnˋvaɪrənmənt] (n.) 環境

We must all work together to protect the environment.
我們得通力合作來保護環境。

◆□⁶⁵⁷ **episode** [ˋɛpəˌsod] (n.) 一集

I tape every episode of *Friends* so that I can watch it over and over again.
我錄下了《六人行》的每一集，這樣我就可以重複看很多次。

□⁶⁵⁸ **era** [ˋɪrə] (n.) 時代，紀元

This will be the most famous invention of our era.
這將是我們這個時代最著名的發明。

□⁶⁵⁹ **essay** [ˋɛse] (n.) 文章，短論

We've got to write an essay about the water pollution.
我們必須寫一篇有關水污染的文章。

□⁶⁶⁰ **evidence** [ˋɛvədəns] (n.) 證據

He went free because there was no evidence to prove he was guilty.
由於沒有證據證明他有罪，他因此獲得釋放。

名詞

□ 661 **executive** [ɪgˋzɛkjutɪv] (n.) 高級主管

My uncle is an executive at a big company.
我叔叔是一家大公司的高級主管。

□ 662 **exhibit** [ɪgˋzɪbɪt] (n.) 展覽

I plan to show my handicrafts at the art exhibit this weekend.
我打算在本週末的藝術展覽中展示我的手工藝品。

◆□ 663 **explosive** [ɪkˋsplosɪv] (n.) 炸藥

The warheads contain around 2,000 lb of high explosive.
這些彈頭裡有兩千磅的強力炸藥。

◆□ 664 **exposure** [ɪkˋspoʒɚ] (n.) 暴露

Too much exposure to the summer sun might harm your skin.
過度暴露於夏日陽光下可能會傷害你的肌膚。

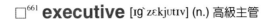

executive | exhibit | explosive | exposure

□ 665 **expression** [ɪkˋsprɛʃən] (n.) 說法

Americans often use the expression "cool" to show approval.
美國人常用「酷」這種說法來表示贊同。

□ 666 **factor** [ˋfæktɚ] (n.) 因素

There are many factors that determine a person's character.
一個人的個性由許多因素決定。

□ 667 **fair** [fɛr] (n.) 博覽會；市集

Many universities attended this year's education fair.
許多大學參加了今年的教育博覽會。

□ 668 **fantasy** [ˋfæntəsɪ] (n.) 幻想

I've always had a fantasy about living in Hawaii.
我一直幻想能住在夏威夷。

N O P Q R S T U V W X Y Z

| expression | factor | fair | fantasy |

名詞

□669 **fate** [fet] (n.) 命運

I never guessed fate would be so mean to me.
我從未料想到命運會對我如此殘酷。

◆□670 **fatigue** [fə`tig] (n.) 疲勞，疲倦

Ginseng is good for getting rid of fatigue.
人參有助於消除疲勞。

□671 **feast** [fist] (n.) 宴會

We had a real feast on Thanksgiving.
我們在感恩節有一場盛宴。

◆□672 **feat** [fit] (n.) 壯舉

Climbing to the top of Jade Mountain is quite a feat.
登上玉山山頂是項了不起的壯舉。

| fate | fatigue | feast | feat |

□ 673 **feedback** [ˈfid,bæk] (n.) 反應；回饋

Companies often send out surveys to get feedback on their products.
公司經常寄出調查問卷以取得關於產品的反應。

□ 674 **festival** [ˈfɛstəvl] (n.) 節慶

The water festival is held once a year in Thailand.
潑水節每年一次在泰國舉行。

□ 675 **figure** [ˈfɪgjɚ] (n.) 身材

Her tall, beautiful figure drove men crazy.
她高䠷美麗的身材令男人瘋狂。

□ 676 **fitness** [ˈfɪtnɪs] (n.) 體能狀況

I go to the gym in order to improve my fitness.
我上健身房以改善體能。

feedback　festival　figure　fitness

□ 677 **final** [ˋfaɪnl] (n.) 決賽

The Wimbledon finals are this Saturday and Sunday.
溫布敦網球賽的決賽在本週六、日。

□ 678 **flavor** [ˋflevɚ] (n.) 口味

This store has 32 different flavors of ice cream.
這家店有三十二種不同口味的冰淇淋。

□ 679 **focus** [ˋfokəs] (n.) 焦點

This picture is terribly out of focus.
這張照片極度失焦。

□ 680 **formation** [fɔrˋmeʃən] (n.) 形狀；形成

Cloud formations often look like animals.
雲的形狀常常看來很像動物。

| final | flavor | focus | formation |

□⁶⁸¹ **formula** [ˋfɔrmjələ] (n.) 配方；公式

Love, patience, and understanding make up the formula for a good marriage.
愛、耐心與諒解是組成幸福婚姻的配方。

□⁶⁸² **fortune** [ˋfɔrtʃən] (n.) 大筆錢財，財富

The gambler lost a fortune in Macao.
這個賭徒在澳門輸了一大筆錢。

□⁶⁸³ **foundation** [faʊnˋdeʃən] (n.) 基金會

My father works for the Rockefeller Foundation in New York.
我父親在紐約的洛克斐勒基金會工作。

□⁶⁸⁴ **founder** [ˋfaʊndɚ] (n.) 創辦人

The company's founder retired in 1903.
這家公司的創辦人於一九○三年退休。

N
O
P
Q
R
S
T
U
V
W
X
Y
Z

formula   fortune   foundation   founder

名詞

◆□⁶⁸⁵ **fraud** [frɔd] (n.) 騙人的東西；詐欺

This hair-restorer is a fraud; I'm as bald as ever.

這生髮劑是騙人的東西，我還是和從前一樣禿頭。

◆□⁶⁸⁶ **fusion** [ˈfjuʒən] (n.) 融合

In Taipei you can see a fusion of Eastern and Western cultures.

在台北可以看到東西方文化的融合。

□⁶⁸⁷ **galaxy** [ˈgæləksɪ] (n.) 星系，銀河

Astronomers discovered one of the most distant galaxies known.

天文學家們發現一個已知最遙遠的星系。

◆□⁶⁸⁸ **gear** [gɪr] (n.) 裝備

We need more biking gear before we go on the bike tour.

在我們的腳踏車之旅出發前，需要準備更多的腳踏車裝備。

| fraud | fusion | galaxy | gear |

□ 689 **generation** [ˌdʒɛnəˋreʃən] (n.) 同時代的人；一代

People of my generation have never been in a war.

我這一代的人從未打過仗。

◆ □ 690 **germ** [dʒɜm] (n.) 細菌

Cover your mouth when you cough. You don't want to spread any germs.

咳嗽的時候要摀住嘴巴，才不會散播細菌。

□ 691 **glance** [glæns] (n.) 一瞥

After a glance, I could tell she was not the woman I was sent to find.

看一眼之後，我就知道她不是我奉派來找的那個女人。

◆ □ 692 **glimpse** [glɪmps] (n.) 一瞥

I got a glimpse of the new secretary. She's hot!

我剛剛瞥了新祕書一眼，她真性感！

A
B
C
D
E
F
G
H
I
J
K
L
M

□⁶⁹³ **globe** [glob] (n.) 地球；球

"Okay" is the most widely recognized word around the globe.
OK 是全球最多人認識的字。

□⁶⁹⁴ **goal** [gol] (n.) 目標

His goals are so high that I don't think he can reach them.
他的目標太高，我認為他無法達成。

□⁶⁹⁵ **gossip** [ˈgɑsəp] (n.) 閒話

There is nothing but meaningless gossip in that movie magazine.
那本電影雜誌裡只有無聊的閒話。

◆□⁶⁹⁶ **gourmet** [ˈgʊrme] (n.) 美食家

I'm no gourmet, but I can't eat instant noodles every day.
我不是美食家，但也不能天天吃泡麵。

| globe | goal | gossip | gourmet |

□ 697 **grounds** [graʊndz] (n.) 房屋四周的土地和花園

After graduation, I walked around the university grounds with my parents.
畢業典禮後，我和父母在大學校園內散步。

◆□ 698 **guesthouse** [ˈgɛst,haʊs] (n.) 賓館

We need to find the cheapest guesthouse in town.
我們要找到鎮上最便宜的賓館。

◆□ 699 **guide** [gaɪd] (n.) 指南

Guides to many cities around the world can be found on the Internet.
網路上可以找到世界許多城市的指南。

□ 700 **habitat** [ˈhæbə,tæt] (n.) 動物的棲息地

The waters around Taiwan are the natural habitat of many fishes.
台灣附近的水域是許多魚類的天然棲息地。

| grounds | guesthouse | guide | habitat |

□⁷⁰¹ **harmony** [ˈhɑrmənɪ] (n.) 和諧

In Singapore, people of different races and backgrounds live in perfect harmony.
在新加坡，不同種族、背景的人很和諧地生活在一起。

□⁷⁰² **horizon** [həˈraɪzn̩] (n.) 地平線

The setting sun is just above the horizon now.
夕陽現在剛好在地平線上。

□⁷⁰³ **host** [host] (n.) 主持人

She was the host of a famous TV show.
她曾是一個有名的電視節目的主持人。

□⁷⁰⁴ **identification** [aɪˌdɛntəfəˈkeʃən] (n.) 身分證明

You must provide some sort of identification when you rent a car.
你租車時必須提出某種身分證明。

harmony　horizon　host　identification

□ 705 **illustration** [ˌɪləsˋtreʃən] (n.) 插圖

My daughter likes to read books with good illustrations.
我女兒喜歡閱讀插圖很棒的書。

□ 706 **illustrator** [ˋɪləsˏtretə] (n.) 插畫家

I hope to become a magazine illustrator when I grow up.
我希望長大後能成為一位雜誌插畫家。

□ 707 **immigrant** [ˋɪməgrənt] (n.)（移入的）移民

The Thai immigrants started importing Thai food products into America.
泰國移民開始將泰式料理引入美國。

□ 708 **impact** [ˋɪmpækt] (n.) 衝擊

This new theory will have a strong impact on accepted theories.
這個新理論將對舊理論造成強烈的衝擊。

名詞

□709 **incident** [ˈɪnsədənt] (n.) 事件;事故

Losing my job is an incident that I'd rather forget.
丟掉工作是我不願再記起的事。

□710 **individual** [ˌɪndəˈvɪdʒʊəl] (n.) 個人

A society is made up of many individuals.
社會是由許多的個人組成的。

□711 **ingredient** [ɪnˈgridɪənt] (n.) 成分

Sugar is the most important ingredient in this recipe.
糖是這份食譜中最重要的成分。

□712 **injury** [ˈɪndʒərɪ] (n.) 傷害

To prevent injury, it's best to stretch before exercising.
為了避免傷害,運動前最好先做伸展操。

| incident | individual | ingredient | injury |

♦□⁷¹³ **inquiry** [ˋɪnkrərɪ] (n.) 詢問

The police came and made inquiries about the stolen car.
警察來過，詢問了一下汽車失竊的事。

□⁷¹⁴ **insecurity** [͵ɪnsɪˋkjʊrətɪ] (n.) 不安全

She feels a strong sense of insecurity whenever her husband is away.
她丈夫不在的時候，她就會有強烈的不安全感。

□⁷¹⁵ **inspiration** [͵ɪnspəˋreʃən] (n.) 啟發，靈感

I get the inspiration for my paintings from nature.
我從大自然中獲得作畫的靈感。

♦□⁷¹⁶ **intensity** [ɪnˋtɛnsətɪ] (n.) 激烈

The intensity of the competition makes it hard to make a profit.
競爭的激烈使得獲利相當困難。

N O P Q R S T U V W X Y Z

inquiry | insecurity | inspiration | intensity

「字」我挑戰 9

解答請見 p. 290

_____ 1. The _____ of the cake mix were printed on the package.
(A) episodes
(B) ingredients
(C) issues
(D) feasts

_____ 2. In Taiwan, the Dragon Boat _____ is one of the biggest celebrations of the year.
(A) Final
(B) Gourmet
(C) Incident
(D) Festival

_____ 3. "What's the biggest _____ in your success?" the reporter asked the businessman.
(A) despair
(B) environment
(C) formation
(D) factor

_____ 4. Many of the world's poorest countries have large national _____ .
(A) figures
(B) items
(C) debts
(D) horizons

_____ 5. The children were excited about the dinosaur _____ at the museum.
(A) exhibit
(B) host
(C) generation
(D) formula

_____ 6. Some artists get their _____ from very ordinary things.
(A) fusion
(B) inspiration
(C) insecurity
(D) glimpse

_____ 7. Bill Gates, the _____ of Microsoft, is one of the world's richest men.
(A) enthusiast
(B) founder
(C) direction
(D) foundation

_____ 8. Because the criminal wore a _____ , the police had trouble catching him.
(A) disguise
(B) pair of wings
(C) fitness
(D) guide

_____ 9. In the 1980's, _____ in computer
science became popular.
(A) grounds
(B) immigrants
(C) flavors
(D) degrees

_____10. Katie, who loves pop music, likes to hear
_____ about her favorite singers.
(A) gossip
(B) exposure
(C) cunning
(D) evidence

_____11. The growth of farms and cities threatens
the natural _____ of many animals.
(A) investments
(B) injuries
(C) habitats
(D) damages

_____12. Everybody worked hard to get done before
the _____ .
(A) decade
(B) effort
(C) deadline
(D) focus

TIME
Basic Words 888

名詞

Chapter 10

717~804

共
348
字

- investment 投資
- issue 議題
- item 項目
- journalist 新聞記者
- lace 蕾絲，花邊
- landmark 地標
- legend 傳說，傳奇
- lifestyle 生活方式
- location 位置
- luxury 奢侈品；奢侈
- lyric 歌詞
- mainstream 主流
- makeup 化妝品
- mall 大型購物中心
- mania 狂熱
- manuscript 原稿，手稿
- margin 差距
- massage 按摩
- match 與…匹敵，匹配
- medal 獎章
- medium 媒體，媒介
- mercy 憐憫，慈悲
- microwave 微波爐
- millennium 千禧年
- misery 不幸，悲慘
- mission 使命；任務
- mixture 混合物
- modernization 現代化
- moisture 濕度，濕氣
- monster 怪物
- mood 心情
- motive 動機
- nap 打盹，小睡
- native 本地人
- neon 霓虹燈
- nutrient 養分
- offender 犯罪者
- opponent 對手；反對者
- option 選擇
- orchestra 管弦樂團
- orphan 孤兒
- outbreak 爆發
- pace 步調
- pal 伙伴，好友
- paradise 樂園
- participant 參加者
- passage（文章的）一段，一節
- password 密碼
- patent 專利，專利權
- peak 頂峰，最高點
- performance 表演，演出
- perspective 觀點；展望
- phenomenon 現象
- philosopher 哲學家
- pinnacle 頂峰
- planet 行星

- plot 小塊土地
- poem 詩
- policy 政策，策略
- poll 民意測驗，民調
- post 職位
- potential 潛力
- prediction 預言
- profession 職業，專業
- profile 人物簡介；側面
- programmer 程式設計師
- project 計畫
- property 特性，特質
- prosperity 繁榮
- public 民眾，大眾
- publicity 宣傳；知名度
- ■ quality 品質，性質
- ■ rate 比率
- rating 收視率
- ratio 比例
- reach（手、活動、心力能及的）範圍
- real estate 房地產
- rebellion 反抗；叛亂
- recession 不景氣，衰退
- recipe 食譜；祕方
- recognition 褒揚；認識
- reflex 反射動作
- region 地區，區域

- relief 放心
- reminder 提醒的東西
- remoteness 遙遠，偏僻
- reputation 名聲
- request 要求

名詞

□⁷¹⁷ **investment** [ɪnˋvɛstmənt] (n.) 投資

Our company has lost a lot of money from recent investments.
我們公司在最近幾次投資中虧損很多。

□⁷¹⁸ **issue** [ˋɪʃʊ] (n.) 議題

Water pollution is an important environmental issue.
水污染是項重要的環境議題。

□⁷¹⁹ **item** [ˋaɪtəm] (n.) 項目

All items in the store are 20% off today.
店裡的東西今天一律八折。

□⁷²⁰ **journalist** [ˋdʒɜnəlɪst] (n.) 新聞記者

The Watergate scandal was exposed by two journalists working for the *Washington Post*.
水門案是由《華盛頓郵報》的兩名記者揭發的。

□⁷²¹ **lace** [les] (n.) 蕾絲，花邊

He bought his girlfriend a pair of red lace underwear for Valentine's Day.
他買給女友一套紅色蕾絲內衣作為情人節禮物。

□⁷²² **landmark** [ˈlænd,mɑrk] (n.) 地標

I like to drive on older roads and stop at all the historic landmarks.
我喜歡在較老的路上開車，並且在所有歷史性地標稍作停留。

□⁷²³ **legend** [ˈlɛdʒənd] (n.) 傳說，傳奇

I like to read American Indian legends.
我喜歡閱讀美洲印第安人的傳說。

□⁷²⁴ **lifestyle** [ˈlaɪf,staɪl] (n.) 生活方式

His lifestyle has completely changed since he won the lottery.
自從中了彩券後，他的生活方式就完全改變了。

lace | landmark | legend | lifestyle

A
B
C
D
E
F
G
H
I
J
K

□⁷²⁵ **location** [lo`keʃən] (n.) 位置

The location of the house near the supermarket makes it very convenient.
這棟房子的位置靠近超級市場，非常便利。

□⁷²⁶ **luxury** [`lʌkʃərɪ] (n.) 奢侈品；奢侈

In Taiwan, having a house in the mountains is a luxury.
在台灣，擁有山上的房子是一種奢侈。

◆□⁷²⁷ **lyric** [`lɪrɪk] (n.) 歌詞

The lyrics of this song remind me of my first girlfriend.
這首歌的歌詞讓我想起我的初戀女友。

L
M

□⁷²⁸ **mainstream** [`men,strim] (n.) 主流

Many people like to follow the mainstream because it is safer.
許多人喜歡追隨主流，因為比較安全。

| location | luxury | lyric | mainstream |

□⁷²⁹ **makeup** [ˋmek͵ʌp] (n.) 化妝品

I think she wears too much makeup.
我覺得她化妝化得太濃了。

♦□⁷³⁰ **mall** [mɔl] (n.) 大型購物中心

We spent ten hours in the mall shopping for
Christmas.
我們為了耶誕節花了十個鐘頭在購物中心購物。

♦□⁷³¹ **mania** [ˋmenɪə] (n.) 狂熱

Pokemon mania has spread across the
world.
神奇寶貝熱潮橫掃全球。

□⁷³² **manuscript** [ˋmænjə͵skrɪpt] (n.) 原稿，手稿

Most writers write their manuscripts directly
on the computer now.
現在大部分的作家都是直接在電腦上寫原稿了。

名詞

◆□⁷³³ **margin** [ˈmɑrdʒɪn] (n.) 差距

The team won by the largest margin in league history.
這個隊伍以聯盟史上最大的差距獲勝。

□⁷³⁴ **massage** [məˈsɑʒ] (n.) 按摩

After working so hard, I feel I could use a good massage.
在如此辛苦的工作後，我覺得需要好好按摩一下。

□⁷³⁵ **match** [mætʃ] (n.) 與⋯匹敵，匹配

No brand can match this computer in quality.
沒有牌子可以與這台電腦的品質匹敵。

□⁷³⁶ **medal** [ˈmɛdl] (n.) 獎章

When I was in high school, I won many gold medals in track.
我在中學曾經贏得許多徑賽金牌。

| margin | massage | match | medal |

□737 **medium** [ˈmidɪəm] (n.) 媒體，媒介

The Internet is the newest communications medium.
網際網路是最新的通訊媒體。

□738 **mercy** [ˈmɜsɪ] (n.) 憐憫，慈悲

Show a little mercy for the employees that worked all weekend.
給週末工作的員工一些憐憫吧！

□739 **microwave** [ˈmaɪkrəˌwev] (n.) 微波爐

You can cook this popcorn in the microwave.
你可以用微波爐來爆玉米花。

□740 **millennium** [məˈlɛnɪəm] (n.) 千禧年

The millennium bug caused problems for many companies.
千禧蟲給許多公司帶來麻煩。

◆□⁷⁴¹ **misery** [ˋmɪzərɪ] (n.) 不幸，悲慘

People say that misery loves company.
人們說不幸有傳染性。

□⁷⁴² **mission** [ˋmɪʃən] (n.) 使命；任務

My father says that everyone needs a mission in life.
我父親說每個人一生中都要有一項使命。

□⁷⁴³ **mixture** [ˋmɪkstʃə] (n.) 混合物

Their latest CD is a mixture of old and new songs.
他們最新的 CD 是新舊歌曲的混合。

□⁷⁴⁴ **modernization** [ˌmɑdənəˋzeʃən] (n.) 現代化

Modernization has also brought new problems.
現代化也帶來新的問題。

| misery | mission | mixture | modernization |

□ 745 **moisture** [ˋmɔɪstʃɚ] (n.) 濕氣，濕度

This machine takes moisture out of the air.
這個機器可以去除空氣中的濕氣。

□ 746 **monster** [ˋmɑnstɚ] (n.) 怪物

Children's books with monsters in them
always sell well.
有怪物的童書總是很暢銷。

□ 747 **mood** [mud] (n.) 心情

He got a parking ticket this morning, and
has been in a bad mood all day.
他早上被開了一張違規停車罰單，一整天心情都不
好。

□ 748 **motive** [ˋmotɪv] (n.) 動機

What is your motive for wanting to go
abroad?
你想要出國的動機是什麼？

moisture　　monster　　mood　　motive

□⁷⁴⁹ **nap** [næp] (n.) 打盹，小睡

I am going to go and take a little nap.
我要離開並小睡一下。

□⁷⁵⁰ **native** [ˋnetɪv] (n.) 本地人

I am a native of Taiwan.
我是台灣本地人。

◆□⁷⁵¹ **neon** [ˋni‚ɑn] (n.) 霓虹燈

Las Vegas has thousands of neon signs.
拉斯維加斯有數以千計的霓虹招牌。

◆□⁷⁵² **nutrient** [ˋnjutrɪənt] (n.) 養分

All plants need nutrients to grow.
所有的植物都需要養分才能成長。

| nap | native | neon | nutrient |

□⁷⁵³ **offender** [əˋfɛndə] (n.) 犯罪者

The judge said that since I wasn't a repeat offender, he'd only give me a warning.
法官說因為我不是累犯，所以只給我警告一下。

□⁷⁵⁴ **opponent** [əˋponənt] (n.) 對手；反對者

To become better at a sport, it is best to play with an opponent who is better than you.
想更擅長一種運動，最好的方法是找比你強的對手切磋。

□⁷⁵⁵ **option** [ˋɑpʃən] (n.) 選擇

Can you tell me what my options are before I decide?
在我決定之前，你能告訴我有哪些選擇嗎？

◆□⁷⁵⁶ **orchestra** [ˋɔrkɪstrə] (n.) 管弦樂團

The Vienna Philaharmonic Orchestra is one of the best orchestras in the world.
維也納愛樂管弦樂團是世界上最好的管弦樂團之一。

offender | opponent | option | orchestra

□⁷⁵⁷ **orphan** [ˈɔrfən] (n.) 孤兒

The civil war is making more and more widows and orphans.
這場內戰造成愈來愈多的寡婦和孤兒。

□⁷⁵⁸ **outbreak** [ˈaʊtˌbrek] (n.) 爆發

My school had an outbreak of the flu last week.
上週我的學校爆發了流行性感冒。

□⁷⁵⁹ **pace** [pes] (n.) 步調

The pace of life in Taipei is very fast.
台北的生活步調非常快。

□⁷⁶⁰ **pal** [pæl] (n.) 伙伴，好友

Tom and Dan are old pals from high school.
湯姆與丹是中學時期認識的老朋友。

| orphan | outbreak | pace | pal |

□⁷⁶¹ **paradise** [ˈpærəˌdaɪs] (n.) 樂園

My friend says that Oregon is a natural paradise.
我的朋友說奧勒岡州是天然樂園。

□⁷⁶² **participant** [pərˈtɪsəpənt] (n.) 參加者

Every participant of the meeting must sign in this book.
每個與會者都必須在這本冊子上簽名。

□⁷⁶³ **passage** [ˈpæsɪdʒ] (n.)（文章的）一段，一節

There were several passages in that novel that I didn't understand.
這本小說中有幾段我沒看懂。

□⁷⁶⁴ **password** [ˈpæsˌwɝd] (n.) 密碼

If you forget your password, you won't be able to withdraw money.
如果你忘了密碼將無法提款。

N
O
P
Q
R
S
T
U
V
W
X
Y
Z

paradise   participant   passage   password

名詞

□⁷⁶⁵ **patent** [ˋpætn̩t] (n.) 專利，專利權

You should get a patent on your new invention.
你應該為新發明申請專利。

□⁷⁶⁶ **peak** [pik] (n.) 頂峰，最高點

I reached the peak of my career when I was 52 years old.
我五十二歲時達到事業的巔峰。

□⁷⁶⁷ **performance** [pɚˋfɔrməns] (n.) 表演，演出

The music performance tonight lacked passion.
今晚的音樂演出缺乏熱情。

□⁷⁶⁸ **perspective** [pɚˋspɛktɪv] (n.) 觀點；展望

Everyone has his own perspective on this matter.
這件事情每個人都有自己的觀點。

| patent | peak | performance | perspective |

□⁷⁶⁹ **phenomenon** [fə`namə,nan] (n.) 現象

A solar eclipse is a natural phenomenon that doesn't occur often.
日蝕是一個不常發生的自然現象。

□⁷⁷⁰ **philosopher** [fə`lasəfə] (n.) 哲學家

Plato is one of the world's best-known philosophers.
柏拉圖是世界最知名的哲學家之一。

◆□⁷⁷¹ **pinnacle** [`pɪnəkḷ] (n.) 頂峰

By the age of forty she had reached the pinnacle of her career.
四十歲之前她就達到了事業的顛峰。

□⁷⁷² **planet** [`plænɪt] (n.) 行星

How many people live on our planet?
有多少人居住在我們的星球上？

N O **P** Q R S T U V W X Y Z

□[773] **plot** [plɑt] (n.) 小塊土地

We chose a plot of land near the lake to build our house on.
我們選擇了湖濱的這片土地建造房子。

□[774] **poem** [ˈpoɪm] (n.) 詩

I used to write poems for my girlfriend.
我以前常寫詩給女友。

□[775] **policy** [ˈpɑləsɪ] (n.) 政策，策略

Our company's policy is that the customer is always right.
我們公司的政策是：顧客永遠是對的。

□[776] **poll** [pol] (n.) 民意測驗，民調

Public polls show that most people watch six hours or more of TV a day.
民調顯示，大多數人一天花六個小時以上的時間看電視。

□⁷⁷⁷ **post** [post] (n.) 職位

My husband is going to accept a teaching post in Africa.
我丈夫將要接受非洲的一項教職。

□⁷⁷⁸ **potential** [pə`tɛnʃəl] (n.) 潛力

I feel I have a lot of unrealized potential.
我覺得自己具有許多尚未發掘的潛力。

◆□⁷⁷⁹ **prediction** [prɪ`dɪkʃən] (n.) 預言

Do you have any predictions about what will happen next year?
你可以預言明年會發生什麼事嗎？

□⁷⁸⁰ **profession** [prə`fɛʃən] (n.) 職業；專業

Medicine is a high-paying profession.
醫療是高收入的行業。

N O P Q R S T U V W X Y Z

| post | potential | prediction | profession |

◆□781 **profile** [ˋprofaɪl] (n.) 人物簡介；側面

Have you checked the exclusive profile of the new tennis champion?
你看了新網球冠軍的獨家人物介紹了嗎？

□782 **programmer** [ˋprogræmɚ] (n.) 程式設計師

My uncle is a computer programmer in Silicon Valley.
我舅舅是矽谷裡的一位電腦程式設計師。

□783 **project** [ˋprodʒɛkt] (n.) 計畫

I'm going to be the leader of a new project.
我將擔任一項新計畫的領導人。

□784 **property** [ˋpropɚtɪ] (n.) 特性，特質

Gold has the unique property of being resistant to rust.
黃金具有抗鏽的特性。

☐ ⁷⁸⁵ **prosperity** [prɑsˋpɛrətɪ] (n.) 繁榮

The war was followed by a long period of peace and prosperity.
戰後有一段很長的和平與繁榮。

☐ ⁷⁸⁶ **public** [ˋpʌblɪk] (n.) 民眾，大眾

The public watched the president on TV.
民眾看到總統出現在電視上。

◆ ☐ ⁷⁸⁷ **publicity** [pʌbˋlɪsətɪ] (n.) 宣傳；知名度

The President's visit gave the teahouse the best publicity it could dream for.
總統的到訪，讓這家茶藝館得到夢魅以求的最佳宣傳。

☐ ⁷⁸⁸ **quality** [ˋkwɑlətɪ] (n.) 品質，性質

The quality of air in Taipei is terrible.
台北的空氣品質很糟。

A
B
C
D
E
F
G
H
I
J
K
L
M

□⁷⁸⁹ **rate** [ret] (n.) 比率

The Central Bank lowered interest rates again today.
中央銀行今天再度調降利率。

□⁷⁹⁰ **rating** [ˋretɪŋ] (n.) 收視率

That TV series has received extremely high ratings.
那部電視影集有極高的收視率。

□⁷⁹¹ **ratio** [ˋreʃo] (n.) 比例

The ratio of women to men in the world is about one to one.
世界上男女的比例約為一比一。

□⁷⁹² **reach** [ritʃ] (n.) （手、活動、心力能及的）範圍

Put that bottle of weed-killer out of the reach of the children.
把那瓶除草劑放在小孩不能拿到的地方。

| rate | rating | ratio | reach |

□⁷⁹³ **real estate** [ˈriəl əˈstet] (n.) 房地產

Real estate in Taipei is incredibly expensive.
台北的房地產貴得不可思議。

◆□⁷⁹⁴ **rebellion** [rɪˈbɛljən] (n.) 反抗；叛亂

In college, he was the leader of a student rebellion.
在大學時，他是學生反抗運動的領導人物。

◆□⁷⁹⁵ **recession** [rɪˈsɛʃən] (n.) 不景氣，衰退

The recession is causing a lot of unemployment these days.
最近的不景氣造成很多失業人口。

□⁷⁹⁶ **recipe** [ˈrɛsəpɪ] (n.) 食譜；祕方

Mom's recipe for apple pie includes four green apples.
母親的蘋果派食譜包括四顆青蘋果。

real estate | rebellion | recession | recipe

名詞

◆ □⁷⁹⁷ **recognition** [ˌrɛkəɡˋnɪʃən] (n.) 褒揚;認識

He finally received some recognition for all the work he has done.
他做了這麼多的事,終於得到了一些表揚。

◆ □⁷⁹⁸ **reflex** [ˋriflɛks] (n.) 反射動作

The doctor hit me just below the knee to test my reflexes.
醫生敲我的膝蓋下方來測試我的反射動作。

□⁷⁹⁹ **region** [ˋridʒən] (n.) 地區,區域

Tuscany is the most romantic region in Italy.
突斯坎尼是義大利最浪漫的地區。

□⁸⁰⁰ **relief** [rɪˋlif] (n.) 放心

I felt a huge sense of relief when I found out I had passed the test.
當我知道已通過了考試,感到大為放心。

| recognition | reflex | region | relief |

◆□⁸⁰¹ **reminder** [rɪˋmaɪndə] (n.) 提醒的東西

Just as a reminder, that proposal needs to
be finished by Friday.
順帶提醒，那份提案必須在星期五以前完成。

□⁸⁰² **remoteness** [rɪˋmotnɪs] (n.) 遙遠，偏僻

The remoteness of the town meant that
medical care was difficult to come by.
這個市鎮的偏遠位置意味著醫療服務不易取得。

□⁸⁰³ **reputation** [ˌrɛpjəˋteʃən] (n.) 名聲

He has a reputation for getting things done
on time.
他以能準時完成任務而聞名。

□⁸⁰⁴ **request** [rɪˋkwɛst] (n.) 要求

Let me know if you have any requests.
如果你有任何要求就讓我知道。

N
O
P
Q
R
S
T
U
V
W
X
Y
Z

reminder | remoteness | reputation | request

「字」我挑戰 10

解答請見 p. 290

_____ 1. Central banks in many countries raise and lower interest _____ to help the economy.
(A) rates
(B) options
(C) ratings
(D) risks

_____ 2. The mountain gorilla is a _____ of central Africa's highlands.
(A) pal
(B) location
(C) project
(D) native

_____ 3. On weekends, this _____ is usually very crowded.
(A) real estate
(B) mainstream
(C) mall
(D) participant

_____ 4. The actor considered winning an Oscar the _____ of his career.
(A) performance
(B) pinnacle
(C) profession
(D) request

_____ 5. Professor Chen gave her students a
_____ that their papers were due on
Monday.
(A) mission
(B) reminder
(C) motive
(D) recognition

_____ 6. When the _____ appeared on the
screen, everyone screamed.
(A) philosopher
(B) professional
(C) public
(D) monster

_____ 7. In Taipei City, the Grand Hotel is a major
_____ .
(A) passage
(B) landmark
(C) margin
(D) password

_____ 8. Thomas Edison had _____ for a large
number of inventions.
(A) nutrients
(B) patents
(C) programmers
(D) legends

_____ 9. Army forces quickly put down the_____.
    (A) rebellion
    (B) manuscript
    (C) phenomenon
    (D) publicity

_____10. _____ taken before the election
    indicated the likely winner.
    (A) Ratios
    (B) Mixtures
    (C) Polls
    (D) Medals

_____11. Kyle had a hard time keeping up with the
    _____ of work at his new job.
    (A) orphan
    (B) lifestyle
    (C) medium
    (D) pace

_____12. At the turn of the _____ , millions of
    people around the world celebrated.
    (A) planet
    (B) millennium
    (C) prosperity
    (D) lyric

TIME

Basic Words 888

名詞	Chapter 11
805~888

共
348
字

□ resident　居民
□ rider　騎士；乘客
□ rifle　來福槍
□ risk　風險
□ rival　對手，競爭者
□ role　角色
□ romance　戀情，羅曼史
□ rubber　橡膠
□ ruin　遺跡，廢墟
■ scandal　醜聞
□ scene　出事地點；場景
□ scheme　計畫；詭計
□ score　分數
□ screen　螢幕
□ secret agent　間諜，情報員
□ section　部分，一段
□ sensation　轟動的人或事物
□ sensitivity　敏感度
□ series　系列
□ session　時段，一次
□ settler　開拓者
□ shock　震驚，震撼
□ shortcut　捷徑
□ side effect　副作用
□ sidewalk　人行道
□ silk　絲
□ skeptic　懷疑論者
□ slice　薄片

□ solution　解決辦法
□ spokesperson　發言人
□ spot　地點
□ stability　安定，穩定
□ staff　工作人員
□ standstill　停頓
□ statue　雕像
□ strategy　策略；戰略
□ studio　工作室
□ stuff　東西
□ substance　物質
□ survey　調查
□ symbol　象徵
□ sympathy　同情
■ talent　才華，天份
□ talk show　脫口秀
□ tap water　自來水
□ target　靶子，標的
□ technique　技巧
□ technology　科技
□ temper　脾氣
□ terrain　地形，地勢
□ territory　領土，領地
□ terrorist　恐怖份子
□ texture　質地
□ theme　主題
□ threat　威脅
□ thrill　刺激，興奮

□ thriller 驚悚片

□ tip 尖端

□ topic 主題，話題

□ tour 巡迴；觀摩

□ trace 蹤跡

□ track 蹤跡，軌道

□ tragedy 悲劇

□ trap 陷阱

□ treasure 財寶

□ treatment 治療方法

□ trend 趨勢

□ tube 管子

■ urge 衝動

■ vanguard 先鋒

□ vanity 虛榮

□ variety 種類，變化

□ vegetarian 素食者

□ vehicle 車輛，交通工具

□ version 版本

□ veteran 老兵；老手

□ victim 受害者

□ violation 違反

□ violence 暴力

□ virus 病毒

■ war zone 戰區

□ weapon 武器

□ workout 運動，健身

□ wrestling 摔角

□805 **resident** [ˋrɛzədənt] (n.) 居民

The local residents were angry at the lack of parking spaces.
當地居民因為缺乏停車空間而憤怒。

□806 **rider** [ˋraɪdə] (n.) 騎士；乘客

One of the riders was thrown off his horse.
其中一位騎士摔下馬了。

◆□807 **rifle** [ˋraɪfl] (n.) 來福槍

My father gave me a rifle for my 14th birthday so I could hunt.
父親送我一把來福槍作為我十四歲的生日禮物，好讓我能打獵。

□808 **risk** [rɪsk] (n.) 風險

Using the Internet increases the risk of getting viruses.
使用網路會增加感染電腦病毒的風險。

◆□⁸⁰⁹ **rival** [ˋraɪvl] (n.) 對手，競爭者

I'm your friend, not your rival.
我是你的朋友，不是你的對手。

□⁸¹⁰ **role** [rol] (n.) 角色

What role are you going to play in
tomorrow's play?
你將在明天的戲中演出什麼角色？

□⁸¹¹ **romance** [ˋromæns] (n.) 戀情，羅曼史

They got married last year after a long-
running romance.
在一段愛情長跑後他們在去年結婚。

□⁸¹² **rubber** [ˋrʌbɚ] (n.) 橡膠

Car tires are usually made of rubber.
汽車輪胎大多是橡膠做的。

| rival | role | romance | rubber |

名詞

◆□⁸¹³ **ruin** [ˋrʊɪn] (n.) 遺跡，廢墟

The ruins of Pompeii have attracted tourists for years.
龐貝城遺跡多年來一直吸引觀光客造訪。

□⁸¹⁴ **scandal** [ˋskændl] (n.) 醜聞

President Clinton was plagued by a series of scandals.
柯林頓總統的醜聞不斷。

□⁸¹⁵ **scene** [sin] (n.) 出事地點；場景

Two police cars hurried to the scene of the accident.
兩輛警車趕往事故現場。

◆□⁸¹⁶ **scheme** [skim] (n.) 計畫；詭計

He is always trying to think of a new scheme to get rich.
他總是在思考致富的新計畫。

| ruin | scandal | scene | scheme |

□817 **score** [skor] (n.) 分數

This Website provides the latest scores for all the major sports.
這個網站提供所有主要運動的最新比數。

□818 **screen** [skrin] (n.) 螢幕

My new TV has a 21-inch screen.
我的新電視有二十一吋的螢幕。

□819 **secret agent** [ˋsikrɪt ˋedʒənt] (n.) 間諜，情報員

Paul worked as a secret agent for five years.
保羅做了五年的情報員。

□820 **section** [ˋsɛkʃən] (n.) 部分，一段

Have you finished reading the sports section of the paper?
報紙的體育版你看完了沒有？

N
O
P
Q
R
S
T
U
V
W
X
Y
Z

| score | screen | secret agent | section |

名詞

◆ □⁸²¹ **sensation** [sɛnˋseʃən] (n.) 轟動的人或事物

The new book by J. K. Rowling was quite a sensation.
羅琳的新書相當轟動。

□⁸²² **sensitivity** [ˌsɛnsəˋtɪvətɪ] (n.) 敏感度

A little sensitivity is necessary when talking to people for the first time.
與人第一次談話時是需要一些敏感度的。

□⁸²³ **series** [ˋsiriz] (n.) 系列

Last year I watched a weekly series on Chinese history.
去年我看了一個每週播出一集關於中國歷史的系列節目。

◆ □⁸²⁴ **session** [ˋsɛʃən] (n.) 時段，一次

The psychiatrist charges $200 for a one-hour session.
這位心理醫師每個時段的鐘點費是兩百美元。

| sensation | sensitivity | series | session |

□ [825] **settler** [ˈsɛtlə] (n.) 開拓者

My great-grandfather was one of the first settlers in this area.
我的曾祖父是這個地區第一代的拓荒者之一。

□ [826] **shock** [ʃɑk] (n.) 震驚，震撼

The shock of her son's death left her speechless for hours.
她兒子的死帶給她的震驚讓她幾個小時都說不出話來。

□ [827] **shortcut** [ˈʃɔrtˌkʌt] (n.) 捷徑

There are no shortcuts to learning a foreign language.
學外語沒有捷徑。

□ [828] **side effect** [ˈsaɪd əˈfɛkt] (n.) 副作用

Chinese medicine has far fewer side effects than western medicine.
中藥的副作用遠比西藥來得少。

N
O
P
Q
R
S
T
U
V
W
X
Y
Z

名詞

□⁸²⁹ **sidewalk** [ˈsaɪdˌwɔk] (n.) 人行道

I don't understand why so many people park their motorcycles on the sidewalk.
我不能理解為什麼有那麼多人將機車停放在人行道上。

□⁸³⁰ **silk** [sɪlk] (n.) 絲

All my favorite shirts are made of silk.
我最喜歡的襯衫都是絲製的。

◆□⁸³¹ **skeptic** [ˈskɛptɪk] (n.) 懷疑論者

My wife believes in God, but I'm a skeptic.
我太太相信上帝，我則是個懷疑論者。

◆□⁸³² **slice** [slaɪs] (n.) 薄片

That's your third slice of pie!
這是你吃的第三片派了！

| sidewalk | silk | skeptic | slice |

□ 833 **solution** [səˋluʃən] (n.) 解決辦法

There seems to be no easy solution to the Taipei traffic problem.
對於台北的交通問題似乎沒有很容易的解決辦法。

□ 834 **spokesperson** [ˋspoks,pɝsṇ] (n.) 發言人

Charleton Heston is the spokesperson for the National Rifle Association.
卻爾登希斯頓是美國萊福槍協會的發言人。

N
O
P
Q
R
S
T
U
V
W
X
Y
Z

□ 835 **spot** [spɑt] (n.) 地點

I found the perfect spot to open our new office.
我發現成立我們新公司的完美地點。

□ 836 **stability** [stəˋbɪlətɪ] (n.) 安定，穩定

Getting married gives people a sense of stability.
結婚能帶給人們安定感。

A
B
C
D
E
F
G
H
I
J
K
L
M

□[837] **staff** [stæf] (n.) 工作人員

Warmest greetings on behalf of the staff!
我代表全體工作人員熱烈歡迎各位！

□[838] **standstill** [ˈstænd,stɪl] (n.) 停頓

Work in our office comes to a standstill
every day at 12:00.
我們辦公室的工作每天到了十二點就停頓下來。

□[839] **statue** [ˈstætʃʊ] (n.) 雕像

I wonder if Rome has more statues than any
other city in the world.
我想知道羅馬是不是世界上擁有最多雕像的城市。

□[840] **strategy** [ˈstrætədʒɪ] (n.) 策略；戰略

If you want to win, you need to have a good
strategy.
如果想贏就必須有好的策略。

□841 **studio** [`stjudɪ,o] (n.) 工作室

The photographer works late in his studio almost every night.
這位攝影師幾乎每晚都在工作室裡工作到很晚。

□842 **stuff** [stʌf] (n.) 東西

I have boxes and boxes of stuff in my basement.
我地下室中有一箱又一箱的東西。

□843 **substance** [`sʌbstəns] (n.) 物質

Glass is a hard substance but easily breaks.
玻璃是很硬的物質，但很容易打破。

□844 **survey** [`sɝve] (n.) 調查

What are the results of the survey you conducted?
你進行的調查結果是什麼？

N
O
P
Q
R
S
T
U
V
W
X
Y
Z

studio　　stuff　　substance　　survey

□ 845 **symbol** [ˈsɪmbl̩] (n.) 象徵

In Chinese culture, red is a symbol of good fortune.
在中國文化中紅色是好運的象徵。

□ 846 **sympathy** [ˈsɪmpəθɪ] (n.) 同情

I have no sympathy for people who make the same mistake twice.
我對犯兩次同樣錯誤的人不會同情。

□ 847 **talent** [ˈtælənt] (n.) 才華，天份

That pianist plays well, but he doesn't have any real talent.
那位鋼琴家彈得不錯，但是稱不上真有才華。

□ 848 **talk show** [tɔlk ˌʃo] (n.) 脫口秀

He likes to watch the talk shows every afternoon.
他每天下午喜歡看脫口秀。

| symbol | sympathy | talent | talk show |

□ ^849 **tap water** [ˈtæp ˌwɔtɚ] (n.) 自來水

They say tap water in Sapporo is drinkable and is indeed delicious.
據說札幌的自來水可以喝而且真的很甜美。

□ ^850 **target** [ˈtɑrgɪt] (n.) 靶子，標的

Being good at his job made him a target of jealousy.
他在工作上傑出的表現使他成為被忌妒的對象。

□ ^851 **technique** [tɛkˈnik] (n.) 技巧

There's more to making beautiful music than just good technique.
想創作出優美的音樂，只憑技巧好還不夠。

□ ^852 **technology** [tɛkˈnɑlədʒɪ] (n.) 科技

Computer technology is changing day by day.
電腦科技日新月異。

N
O
P
Q
R
S
T
U
V
W
X
Y
Z

| tap water | target | technique | technology |

□^853 **temper** [ˋtɛmpɚ] (n.) 脾氣

Don't make Alice angry—she really has a
terrible temper.
不要惹愛麗思生氣——她脾氣真的很壞。

◆□^854 **terrain** [təˋren] (n.) 地形，地勢

You need a jeep to drive through rough
terrain.
穿越崎嶇地形得開吉普車才行。

□^855 **territory** [ˋtɛrə͵torɪ] (n.) 領土，領地

Spies work deep inside enemy territory.
間諜深入敵人領土工作。

□^856 **terrorist** [ˋtɛrərɪst] (n.) 恐怖份子

There were many terrorist attacks last
month.
上個月發生多起恐怖份子攻擊事件。

| temper | terrain | territory | terrorist |

□[857] **texture** [ˋtɛkstʃɚ] (n.) 質地

I bought this shirt because I like its fine texture.
我買這件襯衫是因為喜歡它細緻的質地。

□[858] **theme** [θim] (n.) 主題

I have to write a paper for my English class on the theme of freedom.
我必須為英文課寫一篇以自由為主題的報告。

□[859] **threat** [θrɛt] (n.) 威脅

People in Taiwan are still under the threat of war.
台灣島上的人民仍然處於戰爭的威脅下。

□[860] **thrill** [θrɪl] (n.) 刺激，興奮

I really enjoy the thrill of traveling to new places.
我很享受到陌生的地方旅遊時的刺激感。

N O P Q R S **T** U V W X Y Z

| texture | theme | threat | thrill |

名詞

□861 **thriller** [ˈθrɪlɚ] (n.) 驚悚片

Thrillers are her favorite kind of movie.
驚悚片是她最喜愛的電影類型。

□862 **tip** [tɪp] (n.) 尖端

The tip of that knife is very sharp.
那把刀的刀尖很銳利。

□863 **topic** [ˈtɑpɪk] (n.) 主題，話題

You can select any topic you want for your
term paper.
你可以任選期末報告的主題。

□864 **tour** [tʊr] (n.) 巡迴；觀摩

In May, our band is going on an international
tour.
我們的樂團在五月將有國際巡迴演出。

| thriller | tip | topic | tour |

□865 **trace** [tres] (n.) 蹤跡

After graduation, Tom left town without a trace.
湯姆在畢業之後就離開了鎮上,蹤跡全無。

□866 **track** [træk] (n.) 蹤跡,軌道

The police followed the criminal's tracks to his house.
警察循著罪犯的蹤跡到他的房子。

□867 **tragedy** [ˈtrædʒədɪ] (n.) 悲劇

What happened in Pakistan yesterday was quite a tragedy.
昨天巴基斯坦所發生的事真是個悲劇。

□868 **trap** [træp] (n.) 陷阱

A trap was set to find out who was stealing money from the company.
公司設下陷阱要找出偷錢的人。

| trace | track | tragedy | trap |

□ 869 **treasure** [ˈtrɛʒɚ] (n.) 財寶

The museum is filled with many treasures from the Ming Dynasty.
博物館滿是明代的珍寶。

□ 870 **treatment** [ˈtritmənt] (n.) 治療方法

You should talk to your doctor for possible treatments for your constant headache.
你應該與你的醫生談談持續頭痛的可能治療方法。

□ 871 **trend** [trɛnd] (n.) 趨勢

Market trends for Internet stocks are not promising for this year.
網路股在今年的市場趨勢並不看好。

□ 872 **tube** [tjub] (n.) 管子

When I was in the hospital, they put a tube down my throat.
我在醫院時，喉嚨裡被插了根管子。

□ 873 **urge** [ɜdʒ] (n.) 衝動

Whenever I see a baby, I feel an urge to kiss it.
每當我看到嬰兒，就有一股想要親他的衝動。

◆□ 874 **vanguard** [ˋvæn,gɑrd] (n.) 先鋒

The Smashing Pumpkins are recognized as the vanguard of the US alternative rock.
非凡人物合唱團被認為是美國另類搖滾的先鋒。

□ 875 **vanity** [ˋvænətɪ] (n.) 虛榮

Philosophers say that vanity is human nature.
哲學家說虛榮是人類的天性。

□ 876 **variety** [vəˋraɪətɪ] (n.) 種類，變化

Traveling around the world added a lot of variety to my life.
旅行世界各地，讓我的生活多了許多變化。

□877 **vegetarian** [ˌvɛdʒəˋtɛrɪən] (n.) 素食者

I became a vegetarian after I saw how chickens are raised.
我看到雞是如何被養大的情形後，就成為素食者。

□878 **vehicle** [ˋviɪkl] (n.) 車輛，交通工具

There are no seatbelts in the backseats of this vehicle.
這部車的後座沒有安全帶。

□879 **version** [ˋvɝʒən] (n.) 版本

The newest version of Windows went on sale last month.
最新版本的視窗軟體上個月上市。

◆□880 **veteran** [ˋvɛtərən] (n.) 老兵；老手

My grandfather was a veteran of two wars.
我的祖父是經歷過兩次戰爭的老兵。

| vegetarian | vehicle | version | veteran |

□ 881 **victim** [ˋvɪktɪm] (n.) 受害者

The typhoon victims were moved to the local school gymnasium.
颱風災民被遷到當地學校的體育館。

◆□ 882 **violation** [ˌvaɪəˋleʃən] (n.) 違反

Your new proposal is in violation of our agreement.
你的新提議違反了我們的協定。

□ 883 **violence** [ˋvaɪələns] (n.) 暴力

I think there is too much violence on TV.
我認為電視上有太多的暴力。

□ 884 **virus** [ˋvaɪrəs] (n.) 病毒

Don't open any file titled "I love you" because it might contain a virus.
不要打開任何名為「我愛你」的檔案，因為它可能含有病毒。

N
O
P
Q
R
S
T
U
V
W
X
Y
Z

N
O
P
Q
R
S
T
U
V
W
X
Y
Z

□⁸⁸⁵ **war zone** [ˈwɔr ˌzon] (n.) 戰區
Your room looks like a war zone.
你的房間看起來像個戰場。

□⁸⁸⁶ **weapon** [ˈwɛpən] (n.) 武器
The mind can be a dangerous weapon.
心智可以是一種危險的武器。

□⁸⁸⁷ **workout** [ˈwɜkˌaʊt] (n.) 運動，健身
I do an hour workout every morning.
我每天早晨花一小時運動。

□⁸⁸⁸ **wrestling** [ˈrɛslɪŋ] (n.) 摔角
High school wrestling is often very
competitive.
高中盃摔角往往競爭很激烈。

| war zone | weapon | workout | wrestling |

_____ 1. The journalist sent pictures of the _____ to his newspaper.
(A) thrill
(B) section
(C) war zone
(D) strategy

_____ 2. During many sporting events on TV, the _____ is shown on the screen at all times.
(A) score
(B) symbol
(C) rival
(D) talent

_____ 3. This year, Jack has already received three tickets for parking _____ .
(A) solutions
(B) tips
(C) violations
(D) vehicles

_____ 4. For the party, Veronica bought a new dress made of _____ .
(A) stuff
(B) thriller
(C) spot
(D) silk

_____ 5. Do you ever get the _____ to call your
travel agent and arrange a long vacation?
(A) side effect
(B) urge
(C) role
(D) sensitivity

_____ 6. I had a _____ of pizza for lunch.
(A) slice
(B) theme
(C) sensation
(D) substance

_____ 7. 007 is a famous British _____ .
(A) terrorist
(B) settler
(C) secret agent
(D) staff

_____ 8. My favorite _____ from this movie is
coming up.
(A) threat
(B) version
(C) scene
(D) screen

_____ 9. _____ is not the best way to solve an argument.
(A) Ruin
(B) Shock
(C) Violence
(D) Temper

_____10. At the National Palace Museum, you can see some amazing _____ from China's past.
(A) treasures
(B) topics
(C) zones
(D) sessions

_____11. Would you like a _____ of our factory?
(A) workout
(B) tour
(C) shortcut
(D) terrain

_____12. This store sells a great _____ of watches.
(A) trace
(B) variety
(C) virus
(D) studio

解答

「字」我挑戰 1
1. C 2. A 3. D 4. B
5. D 6. A 7. A 8. C
9. B 10. A 11. D 12. C

「字」我挑戰 2
1. C 2. D 3. B 4. A
5. D 6. B 7. A 8. D
9. B 10. B 11. D 12. C

「字」我挑戰 3
1. C 2. A 3. B 4. D
5. B 6. D 7. A 8. D
9. B 10. B 11. C 12. A

「字」我挑戰 4
1. D 2. A 3. C 4. B
5. A 6. D 7. C 8. B
9. C 10. A 11. D 12. C

「字」我挑戰 5
1. C 2. A 3. C 4. D
5. D 6. B 7. C 8. A
9. B 10. D 11. A 12. C

「字」我挑戰 6
1. D 2. A 3. C 4. C
5. B 6. A 7. D 8. B
9. D 10. C 11. A 12. B

「字」我挑戰 7
1. B 2. C 3. A 4. D
5. A 6. C 7. B 8. D
9. A 10. D 11. C 12. A

「字」我挑戰 8
1. B 2. C 3. A 4. D
5. D 6. C 7. A 8. C
9. A 10. B 11. D 12. C

「字」我挑戰 9
1. B 2. D 3. D 4. C
5. A 6. B 7. B 8. A
9. D 10. A 11. C 12. C

「字」我挑戰 10
1. A 2. D 3. C 4. B
5. B 6. D 7. B 8. B
9. A 10. C 11. D 12. B

「字」我挑戰 11
1. C 2. A 3. C 4. D
5. B 6. A 7. C 8. C
9. C 10. A 11. B 12. B

INDEX

ㄉ

E

F

G

J・K・L

N

O

P

U

正確說美語

一套六冊共360則
超實用必學美語情境短句

　　當別人問你 How do you like your coffee?，而你的回答是 I like it very much.，那很顯然《正確說美語》系列是你最需要的一套書了。為什麼呢？因為這句話在問的是「你喜歡喝什麼樣的咖啡？」，不是「你喜不喜歡你的咖啡？」，而《正確說美語》系列共三百六十則的教學單元，正是教你如何避免這類尷尬錯誤的最佳美語教材。

　　《正確說美語》的作者曹和裕博士，旅居美國超過二十年，他將實際生活中遇上的「麻煩」美語──也就是容易誤解原意的美語，以及句子短單字少但就是怎麼也聽不懂的美語，悉數整理在《正確說美語》中，務必讓你聽得懂最基本的生活美語，並得體地應對。

　　相信透過作者的生活美語經驗談，再加上「實用會話範例」及「重點句子整理」兩大學習主題的加強訓練，絕對能讓你放心到處講，隨時說，從此擺脫雞同鴨講的窘境！

■ 作者／Howard W.Y. Joh
　　單書定價／240元
　　1書+4CD（定價／1,120元）特價／680元
　　6書+24CD合購特價／3,600元
■ 購書代碼／ LE-052　LE-053　LE-054　LE-055　LE-056　LE-057
　　1書+4CD　LE-052E　LE-053E　LE-054E　LE-055E　LE-056E　LE-057E

英文發現之旅

最知性的閱讀測驗

　　《英文發現之旅 ❶ 狗牙與錢幣》與《英文發現之旅 ❷ 捉拿龍捲風》是兩本書名好玩，內容有趣的功能性兼知性的英語學習書。從前的狗牙到近代的錢幣象徵著事物從古到今的演變；捉拿龍捲風為你揭露大千世界無奇不有的祕聞軼事。每本書各有十六篇像這樣話說古今，探索尋奇的文章，文章的題材新奇，報導深入。美籍錄音員精心錄製的CD是想加強聽力的朋友們的標準配備；每篇的「By the way（順便一提）」告訴你文章裡特殊字彙的背景與知識；「說文解字」為你拆穿複雜的文法結構；「網站之旅」延續你好奇的探索之心與發現之旅；為了讓你在英文閱讀測驗無往不利，以大考英文學科測驗與全民英檢中級測驗題型為範本精心設計的閱讀測驗──「小試身手」更是不能錯過。考試要高分，求知更不落人後，英文發現之旅請你對號入座，即日起程。

■作者／TFS編輯群
　單書定價／240元
　一書+1CD（定價／480元）特價360元
■購書代碼／LE-049　　LE-050
　　　　　　LE-049B　　LE-050B

英文大觀園

課堂外的另類英文

　　《英文大觀園1柯林燉柳絲雞》和《英文大觀園2我素個大學生》是旋元佑老師在《時代雜誌》中文解讀版別冊《學習時代》的專欄集結。顧名思義，這兩本書的內容是五花八門，無所不包，而且絕對令你大開眼界。最重要的是它們有別於一般傳統的學習內容：沒有必背的單字片語和必做的文法練習，只有必看的笑話謎語和必讀的幽默小品。

　　所以如果你厭倦了中規中矩的英文課文，請翻開本書，看一看精彩絕倫的古今名言。如果你受不了一天到晚寫不完的英文考卷，請翻開本書，玩一玩精心設計的文字遊戲。如果你受夠了單調的發音練習，請翻開本書，練一練饒富趣味的繞口令和打油詩……。總之，如果你想要體驗教室外的另類英文學習法，請翻開本書，因為除了「學英文」，你還可藉著作者幽默風趣的解說，進一步了解英美的社會文化背景，進而真正地享受完整而多元化的英語學習過程。

■作者／旋元佑
　單書定價／250元
■購書代碼／LE-047 LE-048

國家圖書館預行編目

TIME 單挑中級字彙 888 / TIME for Students 作者群作 ;
-- 初版 . -- 臺北市：經典傳訊文化 , 2001[民 90]
面 ; 公分 . -- (時代英語系列 ; 4)

ISBN 957-476-147-9 (平裝)

1. 英國語言 - 會話

805.12   90008527

時代英語系列 004

TIME 單挑中級字彙 888

Printed in Taiwan

資 料 來 源／美國時代雜誌集團 (TIME Inc.) 獨家授權
作　　　　者／TIME for Students 作者群
編　　　　審／Judd Piggott
責 任 編 輯／金亞玄

名 譽 發 行 人／成露茜
發　　行　　人／黃智成
總　　主　　筆／旋元佑
主　　　　筆／梁民康
叢 書 主 任／陳瑠琍
執 行 編 輯／周健嬅
封 面 設 計／陳淑儀
智 慧 財 產／陳湘玲
製 程 管 理／張慧齡・李祖平
行　　　　銷／洪肇謙・張淑賢
網 路 讀 書 會／蕭怡雯・楊惟玲

發　　行　　所／經典傳訊文化股份有限公司
地　　　　址／台北市 106 敦化南路 2 段 76 號（潤泰金融大樓）7 樓之 2
電　　　　話／(886-2)2708-4410
傳　　　　真／(886-2)2708-4420
　　　E-mail／service@ccw.com.tw
製 作 中 心／台北市 116 文山區試院路（世新大學）傳播大廈
郵 政 劃 撥／18734890・經典傳訊文化股份有限公司
登 記 證／局版北市業字第 183 號

法 律 顧 問／國際通商法律事務所(Baker & McKenzie)
　　　　　　　陳玲玉律師・潘昭仙律師
製　　　　版／大象彩色印刷製版股份有限公司
印　　　　刷／科樂印刷事業股份有限公司
裝　　　　訂／臺興印刷裝訂股份有限公司
總　　經　　銷／時代雜誌中文解讀版
服 務 電 話／(886-2)2754-0088
服 務 傳 真／(886-2)2754-0099
零 售 經 銷／凌域國際股份有限公司　電話／(886-2)2298-3838

定　　　價／360 元   書＋4CD／特價 699 元
特　　　價／280 元   亞洲、大洋洲 US$ 35
海 外 售 價／亞洲、大洋洲 US$ 14   歐美非　　　US$ 47
　　　　　　　歐美非　　　 US$ 19

　　　ISBN　957-476-147-9
出 版 日 期／2001 年 6 月 25 日初版
　　　　　　　2002 年 3 月 25 日初版三刷

如有缺頁、破損、裝訂錯誤，請寄回本公司調換。
台北市 106 敦化南路 2 段 76 號（潤泰金融大樓）7 樓之 2
免費服務專線 0800-011-077